Diablo's Double!

Gabi Adam

Diablo's Double!

ISBN: 1-933343-02-8

Stabenfeldt, Inc.
457 North Main Street
Danbury, CT 06811
www.pony.us

*For all those riders who spare their horses
by sometimes going without a ride.*

Chapter 1

"Wow, never in a million years would I have thought that we'd see each other again so soon! It's been only three weeks since we were here last," proclaimed Ricki Sulai, walking to the stallions' stable on Highland Farms Estate alongside her new friend, Gwendolyn Highland. Bringing up the rear were Ricki's best friends and riding companions, Cathy Sutherland, Lillian Bates, and Kevin Thomas.

"Yes, I know," replied Gwendolyn. The horse paradise and stud farm belonged to Gwen's grandmother, Mrs. Charles Osgood Highland III. "But everything was so crazy during your last visit. Granny thought it would be a good idea to invite you all back again. She hopes things will be much quieter this time, and that you and your horses will be able to enjoy the days spent here. As for me, I can think of a thousand other reasons why it's important for me to have you here! I'm really happy to see you all again!"

"We are, too! Trust us!" Ricki knew that she spoke for the group.

The teens entered the airy, bright stable and ran toward

the stall that housed a huge black horse, proud and noble and obviously aware of his unique beauty.

The youngsters had already toured several of the stables on the property, but Gwendolyn had saved the best for last.

"It's hard to believe that we didn't get a chance to see your star stallion the last time we were here," said Kevin.

"We were all just too stressed out!" grinned Cathy.

"See, another reason for you all to come back! May I present... Garibaldi!" said Gwendolyn grandly, her eyes glowing with pride.

"Wow, he looks like a larger version of Diablo," Ricki exclaimed, and then blushed. She'd managed to compare this superstud stallion to her own gelding. "Well, I mean..."

Gwendolyn laughed. "No need to explain. You're right! Your wonderful Diablo could be Garibaldi's brother!"

"Well, if you see the resemblance too, then I'm really happy," said Ricki, smiling. She took her boyfriend Kevin's arm. "Don't you think he looks more beautiful and powerful than he did in the photos that were in the last issue of the *Riding Journal*? I didn't notice the similarities to Diablo then."

But Kevin seemed not to have heard the question. "Oh, man, I don't think I've ever seen such a beautiful stallion in the flesh," he said quietly with a look of pure awe.

Lillian winked knowingly at Cathy and teased, "He's never even *seen* a stallion before."

"You're right," Kevin agreed, "but then neither have you. And for our first, we couldn't do better than Garibaldi. You don't see a magnificent stallion like this every day."

"I do," laughed Gwendolyn, "but I'm sure I have the same feeling about Garibaldi that you all have when you're visiting your horses in their stalls! I think your own horse, the one you love, is always the most beautiful in your eyes, don't you?"

Cathy nodded. "It doesn't even have to be your own horse," she said, thinking of her foster horse, Rashid. She would never trade him, not even for Garibaldi. Every day she was thankful to Rashid's owner, Carlotta Mancini, the retired circus bareback rider, for allowing her to ride the dun horse and treat him just as if he were her own.

Kevin thought of his roan, Sharazan, and had to agree with Gwendolyn.

Lillian, the owner of snow-white Doc Holliday, could hardly keep herself from laughing. "Tell us, Gwen, how many super-beauties do you have at Highland Farms?" she asked. "I stopped counting at fifty."

Gwendolyn thought about that for a moment. "I can't tell you exactly, because there are always new mares, and then some foals get sold ... I think you'd better ask my grandmother. She always knows exactly how many horses are in her stalls or out on her paddocks."

The kids had a hard time taking their leave of the wonderful animal, but Gwendolyn reminded them that they hadn't come for a visit just to stand in front of Garibaldi's stall. "I thought we wanted to go riding!" she exclaimed.

"Of course! And we'd have been well on our way by now if you hadn't held us up by showing us all these stud stallions!" replied Kevin, as the five friends started to leave the stable.

While they were walking over to the stable set aside for visiting horses, where their horses were housed in spotless huge stalls, Ricki thought back to her last visit to Highland Farms Estate ...

7

*

Carlotta's old friend, Eleanor Highland, had invited Ricki and her three friends to spend a weekend with their horses on her stud farm. She had sent a huge horse trailer to pick up the kids and their four-legged friends and bring them there, but on the way, the trailer had two flat tires and the teenagers had to make their way to the estate on their own.

On the way, Ricki suffered sunstroke, and Mrs. Highland's doctor had ordered bed rest for her. However, when Sunshine, Gwendolyn's mare, who was very pregnant, escaped from the paddock and was nowhere to be found, Ricki and Diablo rode off to search for the animal.

Ricki had found Sunshine in a rocky area on a plateau near the edge of a high cliff. The mare was just about to give birth to her foal, but when Diablo approached her, Sunshine, fearful and enraged, rose up, and the two horses attacked each other. Ricki was afraid for the safety of the foal.

To make matters worse, Diablo bolted and ran away, but fortunately Cathy was able to catch him.

In the end, with Ricki's assistance, the foal was born, and Ricki named it Golden Star.

As if that weren't enough adventure for one day, the mare refused to accept and nurse her newborn. Ricki, however, who had spent the night with little Golden Star, was able to get the two together again.

All in all, the visit to Highland Farms Estate had been extremely exciting, and Ricki and her friends were convinced that it was unlikely that the dramatic events that had spoiled their last weekend would be repeated.

"Where should we ride to?" asked Gwendolyn, while the teenagers tightened their saddle girths. "Do you want to go to the ruins of the old fort, or to the old mill? It's really beautiful there! The huge wheel still turns, although the mill isn't used any more."

"Where do *you* want to go?" responded Ricki as she mounted Diablo. "I don't care as long as I don't have to see those cliffs again, even from a distance. I've had enough of them to last a lifetime!"

"And you guys? What do you think?" asked Gwendolyn again.

"It doesn't matter!"

"I don't care!"

"We'll do whatever the majority wants!"

Gwendolyn rolled her eyes and groaned in frustration. "What's the matter, you guys? Can't you make up your minds? And just who is the 'majority?'"

"You are!" Kevin grinned.

"Great! Then follow the 'majority' to the mill! I think you'll like it there." Gwendolyn urged her horse Black Jack to the front of the group of riders.

"Okay, men, follow me," she called happily and rode off. After a few yards, she turned around and was surprised to see that only Kevin was following her; the three girls were still back at the starting point.

"How about us?" shouted Lillian. "Can we come too?"

"Kevin, are your friends always this weird?" Gwendolyn was becoming exasperated.

"Well," he said slowly, "to be honest ..."

"Don't say another word," Cathy warned him as she approached the two, but Kevin ducked just to be on the safe side.

"If you go on like this we won't get to the mill until tomorrow," Gwendolyn laughed, and waved to her grandmother, who was watching her young guests from her office window.

"Be sure to get back home safely today," she called after them.

"Don't worry, Mrs. Highland," shouted Kevin. "We had enough excitement the last time!"

"Well, that really reassures me!" Eleanor Highland mumbled to herself as she watched the four young people ride off. Such a carefree attitude is possible only for the young, she thought and turned back to her work.

*

"You have a really beautiful place here," Ricki said dreamily to Gwendolyn, admiring the scenery. But just then she heard Lillian scream in fear.

"Holy cow! Are there snakes here? I just saw a snake!"

"Where?"

"Here!"

Gwendolyn brought Black Jack to a halt and looked at the ground. "I don't see anything!"

"Are you blind? Up there, just before the crossroad!"

Kevin grinned at Lillian. "Your imagination is running wild again!"

"Man, you're really getting on my nerves! You know I'm terrified of snakes!" Lillian turned white as a ghost,

10

and after Ricki had given Kevin a warning glance, he didn't make any more comments.

"It's probably just a harmless grass snake," Gwendolyn reassured everyone. "But when we get to the mill, it's possible that we might see a poisonous snake. After all, there's a stream that turns the mill wheel."

"That's just dandy! You should have told us that at the beginning!" Lillian was still apprehensive.

"It's not that bad. If you leave them alone, they won't hurt you. Anyway, they've become very rare around here," said Gwendolyn, but Lillian wasn't convinced.

"Do you think *they* know that?" Lillian asked, skeptical, before she guided Holli back in line behind Sharazan. She said a silent prayer that she wouldn't meet up with any snakes.

"Are there any snakes in flowing water? I thought they were only in lakes," said Cathy.

"I have no idea! I don't care where they are. The main thing is that they don't come near me! If we don't change the subject, I'm turning back right now," replied Lillian, and felt a chill across her neck.

I'm never going swimming in Echo Lake again, she said to herself.

"Look up there," shouted Gwendolyn, pointing to a large paddock where about ten horses were grazing. One after the other, the horses lifted their heads as they heard her voice and smelled the scent of the kids' horses. "Those are our yearlings."

"Don't tell me we're still on the estate," said Ricki, astonished. "You have more paddocks here then there are fields around our town!"

11

"Well, you know, we make our own hay here, and with all the horses that belong to the estate we need a lot of pasture-land, apart from the paddocks," explained Gwendolyn.

"How can you keep such a large piece of land under control?" asked Cathy. "I mean, the yearlings, for example, they're pretty far from the stables. Aren't you afraid that one of them will be stolen?"

Gwendolyn was silent for a moment before she answered. "I'm always worried about the horses, no matter where they are," she said slowly. "Especially in the last three months. I can hardly sleep with all the worrying."

"How come?" Ricki allowed Diablo to catch up to the others and looked at her older friend with concern.

Gwendolyn didn't want to alarm her friends, so cautiously she told them what she knew.

"There's a 'horse butcher' operating around here who has struck well-known horse farms in the area, especially going after valuable stud stallions. But he has also killed mares and foals. Sometimes it seems as though it could be more than one man, considering how many times something has happened in the past three months. Haven't you heard anything about it? Oh, you couldn't have."

Silently, the kids shook their heads in shock and sympathy.

"It's been going on for three months? Why doesn't the news report it? Or the riding magazines? That's something people should know about." Cathy was outraged, but Gwendolyn just shook her head.

"Why didn't you tell us about it the last time we were here?" asked Lillian accusingly.

"The police don't want to worry the private horse owners. After all, the man has only targeted large estates up till

12

now," answered Gwendolyn. "Anyway, the police figured it would set off a panic and maybe even cause violence if they caught the guy. I'm sorry I didn't tell you about it before, but with all the excitement about Sunshine and Golden Star it completely slipped my mind."

"That's so awful. People like that aren't normal!" said Ricki.

"And although these criminals haven't been caught yet, you let your yearlings graze so far from the stables completely unguarded?" Cathy said stubbornly. "Well, I don't understand that. If I knew about it, I'd be worried all the time!"

Gwendolyn just shrugged her shoulders helplessly. "If it were up to me –" she began. "I think my grandmother's right: You can't change the way you conduct business just because of a few loonies. But I think Granny says that just to calm me down!"

"Just because it hasn't happened to you yet, doesn't mean it won't happen, "Kevin warned.

"Don't even say that," Gwendolyn pleaded as she prodded Black Jack to move on. "Come, old boy, let's get going..."

As the young horse lovers rode after their new friend, they could easily understand how Gwendolyn felt.

Lillian, who had always dreamed of having her own horse farm one day, suddenly wasn't so sure about her plans. The idea that she'd have to worry about her animals all the time didn't appeal to her at all.

Ricki felt sick when she realized that as long as they were on the estate, Diablo and her friends' horses were also in danger.

Gwen should have told us, she thought, a little reproach-fully. *I would never have brought Diablo here if I had known about this threat!* But she decided to keep this to herself. Gwen had enough to worry about.

*

About a half hour later they approached the old mill. "Wow, that's huge!" Cathy was amazed at the size of the mill's gigantic water wheel.

Slowly the wheel's buckets filled with the water from the crystal-clear stream and then, after half a turn of the wheel, released it back into the stream with a splash.

"Inside, the millstones are still turning," Gwendolyn told them as she dismounted. "Do you want to see? It's not locked."

"Oh, yeah!" Kevin was delighted. He had always been interested in any kind of technology – even ancient types like a water-powered mill used to grind grain into flour. Cathy and Ricki dismounted as well, but Lillian remained in the saddle.

"I'm not setting foot anywhere in this area," she said. "Snakes..."

Her friends laughed.

"Well, then hold on to the horses. But make sure we don't have to walk back home because they get scared and bolt," teased Ricki, putting Diablo's reins into Lillian's hands.

The others did the same and then disappeared into the mill.

Lillian sat a little stiffly in the saddle and had trouble keeping the reins of the horses in order in her hands. Black Jack and Diablo kept trying to turn around and look for their owners.

"Fellas, don't get excited, they'll be right back!"

While the girl, astride her horse, tried to keep the horses together, she failed to notice the two men who were lurking against the walls of one of the dilapidated buildings a few yards from the mill.

"Oh, no! That's all we need," exclaimed the larger man as he stared at Lillian. "Let's hope they don't get suspicious and start sniffing around this whole area."

"Did you see those horses? They're really something!" the second man said. "Especially the black one... he's really tempting," he grinned meanly. Suddenly he gave a start.

"Just a minute ... that's unbelievable! Mac, hand over the photos!"

"Why?"

"Don't ask questions, just do it!" Impatiently he snapped his fingers and grabbed the pictures as his companion took them out of his jacket pocket.

"It has to be here ... Darn, where is it? ... Oh, here it is," he said, going through the photos one by one. Finding the photo he wanted, he gave the others back to the large man and began to study the photo carefully. He kept peering around the corner of the building to get a look at Diablo.

"That's him! That's him! Man, that's Garibaldi!"

"Don't be ridiculous, Cal, that can't be!"

"Here, take a look for yourself!" Angrily Cal Tribble shoved his companion slightly, causing the other man to lose his balance.

"Are you crazy?" snarled the big man, but then he recovered his balance and stared at the horses cautiously. He compared the photo several times to the black horse

15

that was standing beside the mill wheel, and almost had a coughing fit, but was able to suppress it.

"I think you may be right," he murmured, his voice rough. "They actually let these teenagers ride around on their best stud stallion – they really are idiots!"

"It's good to know," grinned Cal, who seemed to be in a much better mood all of a sudden. "That tells me that they're pretty careless with their star. It shouldn't be any problem getting into the stable ... so let's get out of here. The kids'll be back any second and I don't want them to see us!"

Stealthily, the two men crawled away, hidden by the trees. Diablo, who had picked up the scent of the two strangers, gave a high, shrill whinny.

"I'm back, sweetie," called Ricki, as she and the others exited the old mill. She was pleased that her horse was greeting her.

*

When the kids got back to the estate, they took care of their horses first and then led them to a beautiful paddock surrounded by birch trees. Afterward they started off toward the main house, where they hoped to find Martha, the cook, in the kitchen and get a pitcher of her special strawberry iced tea.

"If I'm right, I smelled cake baking this morning," said Gwendolyn with dreamy eyes. "I've never tasted better brownies or peach pie than Martha's. There's nothing more delicious than homemade baked goods, don't you think?" she exclaimed.

16

"Hmmm, cake and iced tea, yum!" Kevin swallowed visibly at the mere thought.

"Kevin is a cake-aholic," grinned Ricki and gave her boyfriend a tender kiss on his cheek.

"Martha will be glad to hear that. In fact, she'll probably insist on you having second and even third helpings."

Happy, the group of riders made their way to the kitchen. Mrs. Highland met them along the way.

"Everything okay with you all?" she asked with a faint smile.

"Of course! We were at the old mill and we even went inside to look," Gwendolyn informed her grandmother, who had already walked away without waiting for an answer.

"Is something the matter?" Gwendolyn called after her grandmother.

The elegant older woman stopped a moment and then turned around. "I'd like to speak with you later," she said somberly, and then she disappeared behind the door of her office.

"That didn't sound good at all," said Gwendolyn, more to herself than to her friends. "I think I'm going to go and hear what this is all about right away. You all go to the kitchen. I'll be right there."

Gwendolyn, who had a feeling something was very wrong, quickly followed her grandmother into her office.

"People, I'm starving! Ever since I heard there might be cake, I haven't been able to think about anything else," announced Kevin as he headed for the hallway that led to the kitchen.

"No one is more of a pig about cake than he is," grinned Lillian, as she, Cathy, and Ricki marched after him.

17

"Hasn't Gwen been gone a long time?" Ricki asked her friends as she washed down the last of her cake crumbs with a large gulp of iced tea.

"Mmmm, yeah," replied Kevin, with his mouth full. "Martha, this cake is super. Can I have –?" Before he could finish his sentence, Martha had placed another slice on his plate.

"Kevin, swallow first. Nobody can understand a word you say," scolded Ricki, but Martha just smiled. She was flattered.

"Go ahead, my boy, if you're still hungry. I have enough here. I baked two cakes just in case."

"Martha, I know my mother would be thrilled if I brought her your recipe for this amazing cherry cake," said Lillian.

"I think *you're* the one who would be thrilled," laughed Martha, putting a second serving on her plate as well. "No problem. I'll write it down for you by tomorrow, okay?"

"Great! Thanks!"

"Gwen wasn't exaggerating when she told us about your wonderful baking," added Cathy.

"Stop it, now. Don't flatter me so much. My head will get so big, it won't fit on my pillow," grinned Martha.

*

Laughter greeted Gwendolyn when she came into the kitchen. But a few seconds later, after they heard what Gwendolyn had to say, every trace of their good humor was gone.

They all stared at the girl, who sat down awkwardly at the table and pushed her plate away from her. She was as white as a sheet.

"I ... I'm not hungry anymore. Excuse me, Martha, please."

"Hey, what's wrong? Did something happen?" Ricki stared hard at her friend. "C'mon, start talking, is ... is something the matter with the horses?"

Gwendolyn took a deep breath. "Not with ours ... not yet," she said softly and swallowed hard.

"What does that mean?"

"Well, while we were gone, the manager of Blackberry Hill Stud Farm called. Last night two of his best foals were attacked. They found them this morning in the stall, with ... with knife wounds in their necks and ... and their flanks sliced open. They don't know if they'll survive ..." Gwendolyn had tears in her eyes as she told them the story.

Ricki and her friends stared at her in shock as she continued. "You have to know that Blackberry Hill is only fifty miles away from us. The manager advised my grandmother to guard the stalls, at least at night, so that something like that doesn't happen to us."

"Oh, no, that's terrible," whispered Ricki, devastated.

"Yes." Gwendolyn sobbed quietly. "But that wasn't the only attack. The butcher also attacked very close by. Granny's friend just called and reported that a mare was cut last night with a sharp instrument, like a knife or something, and she was so badly cut up that she had to be put to sleep. Will you guys excuse me? I feel sick to my stomach." Gwendolyn got up so abruptly that her chair tipped over, and she ran out of the kitchen.

Ricki and her friends stared at each other in disbelief. Their hearts were beating wildly as they pictured what had happened.

"For something so awful ... there's just nothing to say," stammered Cathy.

"What kind of people would do something like that?" asked Lillian in the uneasy silence, nervously jabbing her cake with her fork.

"Will you please stop talking? It's driving me crazy!" pleaded an upset Kevin. He felt his stomach begin to cramp up with fear. "If the horse butcher attacks here, he might cut up *our* horses. Whoever's doing this is insane!"

"I need to go check on Diablo," Ricki said softly.

"I'll come with you," nodded Lillian. The other two teens got up as well.

"I wish we were home right now," sniffed Cathy. "Then at least our horses would be safe."

Kevin stared at her for a long few seconds. "What does the word 'safe' mean?" he asked with a terrified look on his face. "Do you think a two-hour drive would make any difference to a man like that? He can get anywhere he wants to – and quickly."

"Thanks, Kevin! That's very reassuring!" Ricki swallowed hard in her fear for Diablo and for all the other horses. "But you're right," she added as they all ran toward the paddock. "No one is really safe from this horrible person – or people!"

Chapter 2

Diablo, Sharazan, Doc Holliday, and Rashid stood in the large well-maintained paddock and grazed to their hearts' content. Every once in a while they trotted over to the shadows cast by the birches surrounding the paddock and rested for a few minutes, while they chased the flies off each other with their tails.

Ricki bent down and crawled under the paddock fence and ran over to her horse. Surprised by her sudden movement, Diablo gazed at her. If being on vacation meant that his owner came to check on him every thirty minutes, then he wished that this vacation would last forever.

He whinnied softly, and Ricki quickened her pace until she could throw her arms around the head of her black horse and lay her forehead against his with her eyes closed.

"Oh, my boy, if you only knew ..." she whispered to him. "You're all standing here so innocently, and not far away terrible things are happening to other horses. Please, take care of each other when we're not nearby."

Nervously, the girl let her gaze sweep in all directions, but the estate seemed to be an idyll of peace.

Sighing, Ricki patted Diablo's neck and then returned to the others, who were waiting for her in front of the paddock gate.

"Everything okay?" asked Kevin, as his girlfriend came to stand beside him.

Ricki nodded. "Everything's okay," she said and tried to smile, but the boy knew exactly what she was thinking. Ricki wouldn't stop worrying until she was sure that her Diablo was safe again.

Gwendolyn came toward them with slow, heavy steps. "Please excuse me, but ..."

Lillian waved her apology aside. "There's no need to apologize, Gwen. We feel the same way you do. What does your grandmother intend to do about these attacks on the horses?"

Gwendolyn shrugged her shoulders. "I have no idea. I don't think she knows herself yet. But I'm going to spend day and night in the stalls and keep watch, I promise you that!"

Cathy looked a little skeptical. "In which stall? With Garibaldi or with the foals or ...?"

"I don't know. I'll probably take turns with one and then the other. After all, Mario, Chester, and Jim are here too." Gwendolyn was sure that the two grooms and the stable hand would guard the horses at night as well.

"By the way, my grandmother is thinking of having William take you and your horses home today, just to be on the safe side," continued Gwendolyn softly.

Ricki and her friends looked at each other quickly and they gave her a signal that she should decide for all of them.

For the moment, Ricki was tempted to jump up and start packing her bags, but when she saw Gwendolyn's sad eyes, she inhaled deeply and then said slowly, "You don't think we can just go back home now! I think we should help guard the stables; maybe we can even stay a few days longer. After all, we're still on vacation!" Taken aback, her friends stared at her before they nodded in agreement. Real horse people had to stick together.

Gwendolyn looked each of them with tears in her eyes. "That's really nice of you, but ..."

"No buts!" Ricki interrupted her friend firmly. "If your grandmother has no objections, we'll call home and ask our parents if we can stay a little longer." A crooked smile stretched across her face. "Mom and Company don't have to know the real reason. They would all have a fit if they knew what was going on around here."

Gwendolyn's eyes brightened and she smiled thankfully. "You are really four in a million. I'm so glad I have you as friends and that you're here with me right now! Thanks!"

Lillian walked over to her and hugged her spontaneously. "Well, then let's go talk to Granny Eleanor," she said casually, although she felt a bit uneasy.

*

A huge, white, luxury limousine pulled slowly into the driveway of Highland Farms Estate. Inside, a well-dressed man wearing sunglasses and a white suit peered through the darkened windows with great interest. "The estate is larger than I thought," he said to his chauffeur, who was trying to guide the limousine carefully so that no pieces of gravel would fly up and damage the paint of the car.

Suddenly Jonathan von Branden told his driver to stop while he observed five teenagers leading four horses across the courtyard to the stables.

"There he is, Martin, that's Garibaldi! Do you know how long I have waited for this moment?" Jonathan von Branden stared, fascinated, at the black horse and kneaded his hands excitedly.

This stallion was what was missing on his estate, and perhaps one or two foals from his line ...

Mr. von Branden had come to negotiate a fair price for Garibaldi with Eleanor Highland, and he was determined to get the horse, no matter what the cost. He had chosen to ignore Mrs. Highland when she told him on the phone that Garibaldi was not for sale at any price. A von Branden had never taken no for an answer, and up till now he had gotten everything he wanted. This Mrs. Highland would be talked into it. He was determined; Garibaldi would be on his estate in less than a week!

"Let's go, Martin! Drive me to the main house. I can't wait to pay Mrs. Highland a visit," urged the very wealthy von Branden, and behind the sunglasses his eyes took on an almost crazed look as he watched the horses walk past.

*

Ricki put Diablo into his stall and decided to pay a visit to her favorite foal, Golden Star. Then she intended to call home and persuade her mother to let her stay on here a little longer. She would ask her mother to talk to Lillian's and Cathy's parents and also to Kevin's mother, to spare her friends from having to make the extra phone calls.

24

Luckily Gwendolyn had managed to convince her grandmother that every extra pair of eyes would be helpful in keeping the horses safe. Mrs. Highland knew that her granddaughter was right, and finally agreed, albeit reluctantly.

"Oh, all right. But only with your parents' permission," she told the teenagers. "And you have to understand that I can't take care of you in addition to the horses. At the moment I have both my hands full looking after the horses. So, whatever you do, be careful! Don't give me any more headaches than I already have," she announced somewhat sternly. But there was an unmistakable tone of gratitude in her voice as well.

The five teenagers had no problem with that. None of them intended to take any risks or put their own horses in danger.

*

As Ricki ran over to the mares' stable, where, among others, Sunshine was kept with her foal, Golden Star, she had a brilliant idea. She wouldn't call her mother, she would call Carlotta! Rashid's owner – and Mrs. Highland's friend – would have a better chance, and probably better arguments, than Ricki had, to persuade her parents. Perfect! Carlotta would tell them what an idyllic time the kids were having on the estate, and that they wanted to watch the new foal play in the paddock. And she would convince even Ricki's overanxious mother that with the zealous eyes of Mrs. Highland watching over them, the kids would be well looked after.

Carlotta is a dear. She'll know how important this is, thought Ricki as she headed toward Golden Star's stall.

"Hello, little guy. How are you doing? Hey, Sunshine, do you remember me?"

Sunshine came right over to her and blew into her hair in greeting.

Golden Star had hidden himself behind his mother and now he was peering out inquisitively from under her belly.

"Well, little one, what have you been up to? Come here to me," Ricki begged, but the foal just didn't feel like being petted. He began to buck, showing off.

Sunshine turned her pretty head and looked at her son with disapproval. It looked as though she was telling him to behave himself, and Ricki had to laugh.

"Okay, then don't," she said, and stroked Sunshine's neck. "I'll come back later. I have to go make a call and then it'll be time to eat. 'Bye, Sunshine. See you later, Golden Star. I love you both," she said softly and almost bumped into Chester, who had appeared out of nowhere, as she turned to go.

"And who loves me?" grinned the groom. Ricki, startled at this sudden encounter, breathed a sigh of relief when she realized it was the handsome young groom who had let her stay in the stall with Golden Star the night he was born.

"I haven't a clue, maybe you should ask Martha," she said, but Chester shook his head. "Oh, no, Martha likes Philip Hudson, Mrs. Highland's butler. I don't stand a chance. Too bad, she's a really good cook," he said, his eyes sparkling.

"I'm really sorry to run, Chester, but I have to make an urgent call," replied Ricki and hurried out of the stable.

She really had to hurry, because she knew that Carlotta could only be reached until noon, and after that she always helped at a charity flea market. *I hope Mrs. Highland isn't on the telephone,* she thought, as she hurried up the steps and toward the office.

Just as she was about to knock on the door, she heard Mrs. Highland's voice. She seemed to be talking with someone.

"My dear Mr. von Branden," she was saying, "you aren't serious, are you? After all, I have already told you on the phone, that –"

"But my dear Mrs. Highland, what do words mean? You have something that I want. Tell me your price, and I will accept it without another word. How much do you want? A million? No problem! You know, money doesn't mean anything to me. I would spend my entire fortune to get Garibaldi!"

Eleanor Highland was amused. "A million? Seriously?" she chuckled, and von Branden raised his offer at once.

"We can discuss two million, just don't torture me any longer. Give yourself a nudge and say yes. You know that the stallion would have the life of a king on my estate!"

Mrs. Highland was still chuckling. "Two million? That's a very fine offer, Mr. von Branden," she exclaimed with a twinkle in her eye.

"Does that mean that you will agree to the sale?" he dared to ask, and imagined himself finally getting his way, especially since the owner of Highland Farms had a reflective look in her eyes.

"An offer of three million would be even more tempting," she replied, and looked at the man sitting across from her with a disapproving air.

Who does he think he is? she thought. *Garibaldi is beyond value. Even if this man offered me all the money in the world, I would never be willing to part with Garibaldi!*

Jonathan von Branden leaned back contentedly. In his opinion, Eleanor Highland would never be able to resist his offer. "May I see the magnificent animal up close?" he asked with a winning smile, and, reluctantly, Mrs. Highland gave in.

"All right," she said, eyeing the large grandfather clock that stood next to the door. *It's time to get rid of him,* she thought. She was looking forward to the delicious lunch that would soon be served by Martha, just as she did every day around 12 o'clock.

Ricki had stood stock-still in front of the office door eavesdropping on the conversation going on behind it. Now, as she heard the chairs being pushed back, she became aware of her location and raced off.

I have to find Gwendolyn, she thought desperately. *I'm sure she has no idea that her grandmother has a potential buyer for Garibaldi.*

Excited, she sprang down the stairs in front of the house, taking two steps at a time. If only she knew where Gwen was.

"Gwendooo-lyyynnn!" she shouted shrilly as she raced toward the stables. "Gwennn!"

"What's up?" asked Kevin, at the door of the guests' stable. "Gwen is in here with Black Jack."

"Thanks!" Ricki ran in. She wanted to get to the girl before Mrs. Highland arrived at the stallions' stable with her guest.

"There's a guy here who wants to buy Garibaldi! Did you know that?" she exclaimed, completely out of breath, as her friends came to meet her.

"What?" Gwendolyn was visibly shocked. "Where? Who?"

"I have no idea who it is," panted Ricki, and then she leaned over, planted her hands on her thighs, exhausted, and tried to get her breath back.

"Some guy is sitting in your grandmother's office and trying to talk her into it," she told her, gasping for air. "He wants to pay her two million dollars for Garibaldi. And Mrs. Highland said that it was worth thinking about ... or something like that. Anyway, he wanted to go to the stable to have a look at Garibaldi, and she's taking him ..."

Gwendolyn's expression told it all. Without saying another word, she dropped the brush with which she was smoothing Black Jack's coat onto the floor of the hallway and dashed out of the stable.

She can't do that! Gwen thought desperately. *She can't sell our Garibaldi! Not him!*

In a panic, she stormed into the stallions' stable, where her grandmother was standing in front of Garibaldi's stall with a gentleman in a tailored white suit.

Jonathan von Branden had just pulled out his cell phone and, like a satisfied businessman, he was saying, "My dear Mrs. Highland, I really appreciate your acceptance of my offer." Feeling sure of himself, he searched his electronic address book for the telephone number of his bank.

"You're not serious, Granny, are you?" With wide eyes Gwen stared at her grandmother.

"What, darling? May I introduce you to Mr. von Branden. Mr. von Branden, this is my granddaughter, Gwendolyn."

The girl shook her head and totally ignored the man. "Granny, you can't sell Garibaldi! Please tell me that it isn't true," she pleaded desperately.

29

Eleanor Highland looked very serious. She laid her arm lovingly around her granddaughter and looked at her gravely. "You know, Gwen, some offers are extremely tempting, and one has to weigh the advantages of such a deal. And three million dollars for a horse is, well, I'd say –"

Mr. von Branden smiled silkily and interrupted Mrs. Highland. "You see, my dear, I knew you would decide to accept. I am so extremely pleased that we were able to come to an agreement. If it's all right with you, I'll call my bank immediately and ask them to make the transaction for the sum we decided on. If you would just give me your bank account number ..."

Gwendolyn thought her heart would stop beating. Frightened, she looked at her grandmother.

Eleanor pressed her granddaughter's shoulder. "Excuse me, Mr. von Branden, but I hadn't finished speaking." She gave Gwendolyn a reassuring look before she continued.

"I meant that three million dollars for a prize stallion is definitely a tempting and acceptable offer, but – and now please, listen carefully to what I say – not for Garibaldi! As I have told you many times, this stallion is not for sale, not now, not ever! So, Mr. von Branden, please tell your bank director that he can be glad that he is able to work with your three million dollars a while longer and then kindly get into your car and leave my estate. And please, spare me any more phone calls!"

"But, but ... you said ..." Suddenly von Branden's face took on an unhealthy ashen color. With shaking hands, he clapped his cell phone shut.

Mrs. Highland gestured to Mario, who had been listening to the conversation wide-eyed with wonder, to come closer.

"Mario, the gentleman wishes to leave. Please accompany him to his car. Mr. von Branden, please excuse us, but it's time for our lunch!"

With a pleasant nod, Eleanor Highland said good-bye and led Gwendolyn out of the stable.

With a furious glance at Mario – and at Garibaldi – Jonathan von Branden turned around and stomped down the stable corridor.

Just as his employer had requested, the husky groom followed him to his limousine. He waited until the car had left the estate and was no longer in view.

*

"Wow, Granny, that was cool!" beamed Gwendolyn as she gave her grandmother a thank-you kiss on the cheek. "I thought –"

"Really, the things you imagine," smiled Mrs. Highland. "Garibaldi belongs to our family, doesn't he?"

"Absolutely!"

"All right then, but now I really am hungry." Grandmother and granddaughter walked arm in arm back to the main house.

Outwardly completely calm, Eleanor Highland sat down at the table, but inwardly she could still see the crazed eyes of Mr. von Branden. *He won't give up so easily,* she thought. *People like that are stubborn. He'll be back.*

Ricki and her friends came in a few minutes later. "Oh, excuse us, we didn't know that you were already ... we were visiting with Black Jack and Garibaldi," stammered Ricki, a little embarrassed. Mrs. Highland just smiled understandingly.

"Did you want to say good-bye to him?" she asked, as she took a sip of water.

"What do you mean?" Ricki looked at Gwendolyn who was also laughing gaily.

"Hey, you guys ... all clear! Garibaldi isn't going to be sold! But I have to admit that for a while I pictured an empty stall in my mind!"

The friends breathed a collective sigh of relief and sat down to their lunch. "Great!" Ricki beamed, and just for the moment, the incident was forgotten.

The fact that the magnificent stud stallion would stay at the estate, and therefore with Gwendolyn, lifted everyone's spirits and made the atmosphere at the table very relaxed. Martha was pleased when Hudson told her later how the young people, who appeared famished, had eaten everything in sight.

*

Mrs. Highland had decided to bring all of her horses from the surrounding paddocks back to the stalls, much to the relief of the grooms and Gwendolyn.

"The horses just aren't safe in the paddocks any longer. These criminals can attack them at any time without our noticing it," she announced to her employees at a meeting in her office. "We should bring the animals inside. I don't think these savages will be so brash as to attempt to injure them in their stalls. After all, they'll assume that there's an alarm system that would alert the police and have them here in a few minutes."

"What are we going to do about grazing?" asked Chester.

"We'll let the animals out in shifts; the mares for two hours, and then two hours for the stallions, and so on. It's very important, however, that we use only those paddocks that we can see from the house. That means that the southern pasture is completely off limits."

"Right," nodded Mario.

"If everything is clear, then get going," said Mrs. Highland and opened the door. "The yearlings have to be brought in, and the two-year-olds as well. Take the kids with you; they'll be glad to help."

"Okay." Chester gestured to Mario and they left the office together just as the phone rang.

"Let me know when all the animals are in the stalls," Mrs. Highland called after them before picking up the receiver.

"Yes?" she responded absently and stared out the window.

"Hello, Eleanor. This is Frances. Can't you answer the phone like a normal person?" said her friend.

"Oh, Frances, it's you again! What is it, dear?" Eleanor Highland fell silent while her friend reported more horrible acts of horse abuse.

"He seems to be getting closer and closer to your area," Frances said worriedly. "Please, take care of your animals. This guy isn't just dangerous, he's completely crazy!"

"Thank you, I'll do my best," Mrs. Highland answered and put down the receiver. The calm and peaceful times at Highland Farms Estate seemed to be at an end.

Worried, Gwendolyn's grandmother wrinkled her brow before she dialed the number for the police station. She had to know what the status was from their standpoint, and so she used the fact that she was an old friend of Howard Algrin, the Sheriff at the local station, to find out.

*

Although the reason for bringing the horses into the stables was more than upsetting, the kids still had a lot of fun helping the two grooms and Jim, the stable hand, catch the young animals. They noticed that the mares were much less problematic than the frisky stallions.

"Just look at that Socrates," grinned Gwendolyn. "I can't wait to see if Mario can get him on a lead."

"Want to bet?" asked Chester, who had already caught Commander and Nero.

"Oh, yeah," replied Kevin spontaneously, but Gwendolyn just made a face.

"Think it over well, Kevin. Betting with Chester is like throwing your allowance into the wastebasket! Chester always wins!"

"Allowance?" Kevin acted shocked, and then laughed. "It's okay! I'll bet everything that I have left from my allowance this month. That way, I can't lose much!"

"Oh, no," laughed Chester. "I don't bet with people with no money! I'll make you another offer. If you win, you'll get a free ticket to the movies for you and your friends. But if you lose, you get a free day of cleaning out the yearlings' stalls. We're going to have a lot of extra work, if all the animals are in their stalls. We'll be happy with any help we can get."

Kevin thought it over, saw Gwendolyn secretly shaking her head, and then agreed, laughing.

"Okay, it's a deal!"

"All right, then," grinned Chester and called to Mario. "Hey, buddy, get on with it! I just found somebody to help us clean out the stalls!" As if the whole thing had been a well-thought-out plan, Mario reached out and grabbed Socrates' halter.

"Didn't I tell you?" Gwen laughed, while Kevin tried to estimate how long it would take him to clean out all the stalls.

"That's unfair," the boy mumbled, but then he laughed. "At least I don't have to sweep the seven endless hallways in the stables," he remarked and took Commander from Chester.

"So, then let's go home," said Mario and took the lead with the prancing stallion.

"Are you really going to spend the night in the stalls?" Cathy whispered to Gwendolyn.

"Of course. You will too, won't you?" Gwen whispered back.

"What do you think?"

"Exactly! You guys are as crazy as I am!"

The two girls looked at each other with sad smiles on their faces. Under other circumstances, it would have been great fun to spend the night in the stable.

"What's wrong with you two?" asked Kevin, who was behind them.

"We'll tell you later!" replied Cathy. On the one hand she was glad to be spending the night with the horses, but one the other hand, she didn't dare think about what would happen if the horse butcher turned up at the stable.

"My grandmother can't find out about this, or we'll have a problem!" Gwendolyn told her friend gravely, and then she calmed the young stallion beside her as he tried to break loose from his lead.

Chapter 3

Howard Algrin, the Sheriff, was unable to give his old friend Eleanor much hope. Eight privately owned horses in the general area had been injured in the last three weeks, not to mention the injuries to their stud stallions reported by several of the stud farm owners. And there was still no trace of the perpetrator or perpetrators.

"We're all working as hard as we can, but as of now we haven't had any useful leads in the case," he reported dejectedly. "Riders in clubs and also private horse owners have joined together in groups to patrol individual stables at night. However, they, and the police, always seem to be at the wrong place at the wrong time. We have the feeling that the perpetrators always know where there are unprotected horses. As for the stud farms, most don't have alarm systems. It's strange; the owners have invested a great deal of capital in their horses, but they won't spend a dime on security! It's a real mess!"

After this depressing conversation, Eleanor Highland was relieved when, about two hours later, Chester reported that all of the horses were in their stalls.

"Good," said Mrs. Highland. "Then don't forget to turn on the alarm system this evening, whatever you do! Chester, don't ask me why, but I just have a funny feeling."

*

Jonathan von Branden was beside himself with anger. No one had ever dared to go against his wishes.

"That imperious old witch!" he growled and clenched his fists. Martin, who was aware of his boss's mean temper when he didn't get his way, concentrated on driving. When his boss was in a bad mood, it was better to be silent – and obedient.

"Stop, Martin! Immediately!" The words came from behind him so loudly and so close that he jerked in fear.

"If you'll pardon me, sir, there's no place to pull over," he began carefully, but von Branden just drummed his fingers impatiently on the car seat.

"I said *immediately*!" Von Branden's tone left no room for any contradiction, and Martin's fear of his boss's temper was entirely too great for him not to react now.

"Drive back!" This order made Martin's situation really difficult. He was a good, safe, and reliable driver, but if anything seemed impossible to him at the moment, it was this command from Mr. von Branden.

"But –"

"The next time you say 'but' you're fired! Understand? Let's go! Hurry up!"

Martin nodded in resignation and waited another second before he stepped on the gas, turned the wheel as far as it would go, and shot straight across the road, as though he had just committed a crime and was trying to escape from the police.

Several drivers of cars coming from the opposite direction were forced to make a sudden stop because of the abrupt – and dangerous – turn of the stretch limousine. Yelling and cursing, they expressed their anger.

"It looks as though the rich have different driving rules than other people," shouted one of them out of his window in a rage.

"Hey, who do you think you are?" another screamed angrily.

"Unbelievable! He should be reported! But probably nothing would happen to someone like that!"

"Stop up there," said von Branden, pointing at the driveway of a small parking lot in the woods not far from the Highland Estate.

Lost in thought, von Branden stared in the direction of the stud farm while he lit a thick, expensive cigar.

I just have to have that horse! I have to! It's unthinkable that that woman turned down my overly generous offer! he thought and wrinkled his forehead. In his mind's eye he imagined the row of stalls where Garibaldi would be housed among the other magnificent animals on his estate.

Von Branden sighed. The more he thought about it, the more confused he became.

"Martin, drive me home," he growled at his driver. "And then make sure that I'm not disturbed! I have to think in peace!"

*

The teenagers spent all afternoon preparing for the coming night. They sat together in the corridor of the guests' stable in front of the stalls of their horses, but they couldn't seem to agree on who was going to guard which horses.

"Well, I'm sure that I'm going to stand guard in the stallions' stable," announced Gwendolyn firmly. "It's clear that Garibaldi would be the main focus of any horse butcher. After all, everybody knows he's the most valuable horse on the farm."

"What about the foals?" asked Cathy. "I think they need to be guarded at least as much, especially the foals from Garibaldi's line. If someone were to see little Golden Star, for example, he'd be a goner! And that would be awful!"

"But Golden Star is still so little! I'm sure that Sunshine would demolish the perp!" reflected Kevin.

"These guys don't care about that! If they want to do damage, they will. Sunshine wouldn't stand a chance against them, and Golden Star even less!"

"That's even worse – if that's true then none of the horses is safe. It doesn't matter if it's Garibaldi or the foals, yearlings or mares, carriage horses or guest horses ..." said Ricki softly.

"What did you just say? Oh, heck, you're right! Not even our horses are safe. At the moment they're part of the farm's inventory, so to speak! Well, then it's clear where I'll spend the night – with Sharazan, of course!" Kevin looked at his girlfriend. "And you?"

"Well, where do you think? In the guests' stable, too. Did you think I'd leave Diablo alone?" responded Ricki.

"You didn't need to ask that question, Kevin!" Lillian

nodded in agreement. "Where are Chester, Mario, and Jim going to sleep?"

Gwendolyn shrugged her shoulders. "No idea! I'm not going to let Garibaldi out of my sight for a minute tonight, even if I have to drink ten cans of soda to stay awake."

"Is there soda here someplace?" asked Mario, who had just come in and had heard Gwen's last few words. "I could really use a can!"

"You're too early," grinned Kevin. "With Gwen, soda for staying awake starts getting consumed at ten PM."

Mario looked at the kids a little bewildered. "I don't get it," he said and started to leave, but Mrs. Highland's granddaughter held him back by his sleeve.

"Wait a minute, Mario. We're trying to work out our assignments for guard duty tonight to keep watch on the horses."

"Oh," the groom said. "And does your grandmother know this?"

"Of course," lied Gwen, a little too quickly, and with a fake look of innocence.

"So, no, she doesn't!" Mario shook his head. "Your eyes say you're lying, even if you do look so innocent!"

Gwendolyn blushed. "You know that Granny would never allow that."

"Exactly! Girl, if those bad guys are around, it's much too dangerous for you to run into them! You –"

"Mario, you can say what you want, but I'm going to spend the night with Garibaldi! No matter what you do!" Gwendolyn cut off the groom with her decisive voice.

"And I'm going to stay with Diablo!" vowed Ricki in the same tone of voice. "Nobody can keep me from taking care of my own horse!"

40

Before Lillian, Cathy, and Kevin could even say where they were planning on spending the night, Mario waved them aside.

"You don't need to tell me, I get it!"

Gwendolyn looked at the young man with questioning eyes. "And?"

"And what?"

"Are you going to tell Granny on us?"

Mario didn't respond right away, but looked at each of them intently. Then he said, "No, but you'll have to deal with the fact that we're going to sleep in the stables, too. And if anything out of the ordinary happens, you guys have to go into a hole like mice and wait until it's all over! Do you all understand me?" Mario's expression was stern as he waited for the kids' answer.

"That's fine, boss! We won't do anything we might regret later," Gwendolyn promised, in silent agreement with her friends.

The groom cocked his head a little to the side and tried to read Gwendolyn's mind, but, of course, he couldn't.

"You didn't give me a clear answer," he said, but Gwen had taken Ricki's arm and was already on her way outside with her friends.

"Don't worry, Mario. You won't even notice that we're there," she shouted merrily over her shoulder.

"I'm sure you'll notice me," remarked Kevin before he followed the girls. "I'll be back in half an hour to pay off my losses!"

"Great!" Mario responded. He was pleased that the boy was going to help him clean out the yearlings' stalls.

*

Mac and Cal peered furtively over the wall surrounding the estate.

"Did you see where they brought the stallion?"

"I'm not blind!"

"That's a matter of opinion!"

"Do you have to be so nasty all the time?" Mac looked at his partner accusingly, but he just grinned.

"Before you begin to cry, get to work!" Cal added.

Cautiously, they crawled around the stone wall, every now and then taking a quick peek over the top and at the grounds and its various buildings. Mac was sketching an outline of the premises, which would help them find their way at night.

"Did you include everything?" asked Cal for the umpteenth time. "We can't hang around here forever!"

"Yeah, yeah, but if I forget anything you won't be happy either, will you?" replied Mac, and then he concentrated on his sketch.

"Do you really think we'll be able to find everything later from that fuzzy drawing?"

"Can you do it better?"

"Did I start this job or did you?"

"Oh, shut up, you –"

The two men didn't like each other at all, which was why they were constantly picking on one another.

If Mac weren't so good at figuring out how to shut off all kinds of alarm systems, I'd have gotten rid of him a long time ago, Cal said to himself.

His partner had similar thoughts; *It's too bad he always has such good ideas that bring in so much money. Otherwise*

I couldn't stand how he's always so sure of himself, thought Mac.

"When are we going to do the job with the stallion?" asked Mac quietly.

"It depends on whether or not you're finished with that sketch by the end of the year," his accomplice growled back at him.

"You know what, why don't you just –"

"Pssst ... quiet!" Cal gave Mac a warning glance. "Somebody's coming!"

"Then let's get out of here!"

"How far along are you?"

"What I've got so far will be enough, I think!"

"Okay, then let's get going!" urged Cal. As quietly and invisibly as they had come, they disappeared.

*

"Man, why does it have to be *this* estate? There are plenty of other ones that don't have such complicated alarm systems installed!" remarked Mac about an hour later, while sitting at his workbench and fooling around with his soldering iron and a pair of pliers and a platinum plate.

"Because Garibaldi belongs to that estate, not somewhere else, you idiot!"

"That blasted Garibaldi! Any other stallion would do just as well, wouldn't he?" snapped Mac.

"The boss loves huge black stud stallions, and that's just the way it is!" responded Cal with an ugly laugh. "Now concentrate! If something goes wrong with that thing tonight we'll have an army of policemen on our backs for sure!" Skeptical, he stared at the tangle of cables that Mac was playing around with.

"Are you going to be able to figure it out?" he asked impatiently.

"No problem!" Mac mumbled. "It isn't the first time I've made a gadget like this. The alarm system won't make a sound, I'd bet my life on it."

"That's what the canary said as he disappeared into the cat's mouth," sniped Cal nastily.

Mac threw the pliers angrily onto the floor and stared resentfully at his associate. "You're always questioning my ability! But if this thing doesn't work tonight, it's because you gave me the wrong system number. Where'd you get it, anyway? What'd you do, just drop by, ring the bell, and ask if you could look at the alarm system?"

"Jeez, you're even more stupid than I thought! What difference does it make where I get my information?" Cal replied before he stomped out of the room.

"Jerk," Mac called after him, and asked himself what his partner would do without him. Then he shrugged his shoulders and went back to his work. After all, he was well paid for what he did.

*

"Where are you all going?" Mrs. Highland asked the teens when she bumped into them later that night, several hours after dinner.

"We're hungry," explained Gwendolyn. "I'm sure Martha has some leftovers from lunch or dinner."

"Or from that delicious cherry cake," Kevin added, licking his lips in anticipation.

Eleanor Highland laughed. "Well, I don't want you to starve while you're at my house," she responded. "I think I'd be in a lot of trouble with your parents and Carlotta if you returned home looking like nothing but skin and bones! Oh, by the way, Ricki, you don't need to call home. I've already talked with Carlotta. She said she would talk with your parents and then call me back. I haven't been in the office for a while, but I have an answering machine."

"And?" asked Ricki anxiously.

"You all have a three-day extension," smiled Mrs. Highland.

"What? Only three days? I thought at least –"

"Now child, don't be ungracious. Three days is a lot and, of course, you can all come back again." Eleanor Highland tried to placate some of Ricki's disappointment, but she had no idea why she was really so upset.

Three days ... we can help Gwen guard the horses for only three days, thought Ricki nervously.

"Oh, come on, three days are better than none, aren't they?" Cathy put her hand on Ricki's shoulder.

"Hmm," grunted Ricki and tried to smile. "Thanks a lot, Mrs. Highland. I'm sorry I reacted like that. But it's so beautiful here!" she said quickly.

Gwendolyn's grandmother nodded. She could easily understand the girl. The estate was a very special place for her as well; an oasis of calm and a pure joy.

Mrs. Highland sighed. *I hope it stays that way,* she thought, and got moving again. She wanted to inspect the stables personally before Chester locked up and turned on the alarm system.

"Oh," she called on her way, "don't even think about spending the night in the stables!"

The friends looked at one another as though they had been struck by lightning.

"Darn it!" groaned Cathy with a bright red face.

"Don't worry, Granny, we wouldn't do that!" Gwendolyn shouted in reply, and began shoving the others into the kitchen, where they talked Martha into giving them all kinds of wonderful snacks and drinks.

"You know, the night's going to be long, and we want to get together in one of our rooms and tell each other ghost stories," explained Gwendolyn. She avoided looking Martha in the eyes.

"Oh, can we grab some coke? We wouldn't want to fall asleep during the ghost story marathon," pleaded Kevin, smiling broadly at the heavy-set woman.

"You can do whatever you want," laughed Martha. "The refrigerator is full. Bread is over there, and if you go into the pantry you'll find a large basket that you can put everything into."

"Great! Thanks, Martha," said Gwendolyn, and was relieved when the cook left and they were free to do as they liked. "Let's get going. Just pack everything you can get your hands on. We can sort it all out later."

*

It was almost dark outside. The kids carried their food into the stallions' stable and were now sitting way in the back of the feed-storage area, dividing up their loot.

"I'm never hungry at night," claimed Ricki, so she put

the two rolls and the thick slices of salami Gwendolyn had given her back into the basket.

"Well, if Ricki doesn't want anything, I wouldn't say no to an extra roll." Kevin grinned.

"You're such a pig," laughed Lillian, as she took one caramel after another out of the bag, which was already almost empty.

"You should talk." Cathy grabbed a bottle of mineral water and two apples.

"Are they for you or for Rashid?" Gwendolyn wanted to know.

"Why?"

"Well, if they're for your horse, maybe you should take some more things for you."

Cathy pointed to her overflowing jacket pockets.

"No more room!" she answered. "I'm afraid Rashid will have to share with me."

"I thought you were going to sleep in the mares' stall?" Lillian asked, surprised.

"I am, but I'm going to say goodnight to Rashid first."

"Oh!"

"People, we have to hurry," warned Gwendolyn. "Mario said that we have to be in the stalls before ten o'clock. That's when the doors are locked and the alarm system is turned on. It stays on until five in the morning. Remember, you can't touch the doors during that time or unlock them and go outside, otherwise we'll have the police here in a matter of minutes."

"What would happen if someone really had to go into the stalls at night?" Cathy asked.

"Usually that would be the grooms, the stable hands, the

driver, or my grandmother, and they all know how to shut off the alarm system."

"Do you know how too?" Kevin wanted to know.

"Not really," admitted Gwendolyn. "I do know where all those zillions of switches are that are used to program the system, but don't ask me which ones you have to press when, or how the whole thing works."

"What happens if one of us has to go to the bathroom at night?" Lillian looked around, worried. "Just thinking about it makes me feel like I have to go!"

Gwendolyn laughed. "Don't panic, Lillian. There's a little bathroom behind each saddle room. You won't need diapers tonight!"

"Thank heavens!" Lillian sighed in relief. "In that case, you can give me two more soda cans!"

After everything had been divided up, the five friends got up and looked gravely at each other. The exhilarating feeling of adventure that they had been having was replaced with a vague feeling of unease.

"Let's go," said Kevin softly as he put his arm lightly around Ricki's shoulders.

"See you tomorrow morning – hopefully in good moods." Lillian tried to sound lighthearted.

"So long," called Cathy quietly, as they all said good-bye to Gwendolyn.

"Be careful," Gwen murmured, and she carefully closed the door after her friends.

Not five minutes later Mario appeared and sat down beside her on a bale of straw.

"So where's all that coke you were going to bring?" he asked the sixteen-year-old, who looked up at him, startled.

"Darn, I forgot! Well, I can offer you a sandwich!" she said embarrassed.

Mario laughed. "Thanks, maybe I'll take you up on your offer later! If you want some juice, I have a thermos in the saddle room."

"Mario, you're great! I'm going to get some. Want some too?" Gwendolyn jumped up.

"Oh, yeah, thanks! It's going to be a long night. And it probably won't be the only one," he remarked, and then he got up and walked over to Garibaldi's stall.

"Hi, old boy," he spoke softly. "If you knew why we were here you wouldn't look so self-satisfied!" Lovingly he patted the stallion between the ears and stopped only when he heard Gwendolyn coming back down the corridor.

*

Lillian disappeared into the yearlings' stable, where she was expected by Jim, the stable hand. Mario had told his colleagues that the kids were going to spend the night with the horses.

At first he wasn't happy that one of the girls would be spending the night with him in the yearlings' stall. "Mrs. Highland won't like it," Jim responded.

However, when Lillian came in, good-natured and greeting him with a large piece of chocolate, Jim's misgivings vanished. Maybe it would be better to have someone to talk to, rather than having to spend the next seven hours by himself.

*

Cathy had made herself comfortable behind Golden Star's stall and was waiting for Chester, who would join her there soon.

Actually, I got the best deal, she thought, as she glanced lovingly at Sunshine's foal. Chester is the nicest one, and the most fun! The night won't be boring,

*

Ricki and Kevin waited in the shadow of the stallions' stable until Lillian and Cathy disappeared behind the doors of their lookout positions. Then they started off toward the guests' stalls. They hurried across the cleanly swept floor and jumped when they heard Sharazan and Diablo greet them with happy whinnies.

"Pssssst!! Be quiet!" begged Ricki, but she grinned from ear to ear when Diablo stroked her whole face with his warm, moist muzzle.

"Everything's okay, sweetie," she said, and tried to get him to stop his somewhat overenthusiastic greeting by shoving a treat into his mouth.

Kevin bribed Sharazan with a carrot, which he broke in several pieces so that Holli, Rashid, and Black Jack could also get their share.

"I thought Cathy wanted to share an apple with Rashid," remembered Ricki, but Kevin just shook his head and grinned.

"Chester probably told her she can't go out anymore," he responded.

"Actually, it's kinda nice to be out here together, just the two of us for a change!" Ricki smiled at Kevin.

"Hmm," was the boy's only response, and Ricki, a little disappointed, made a face. "Is that all you have to say?" she asked him as she opened the door to the empty stall next to Black Jack's.

"I was just wondering if it wouldn't have been better to sleep in one of the main stalls. You can tell that no one thinks that anything will happen to one of *our* horses, otherwise one of the hands would have been assigned to guard duty here," he explained.

Ricki sighed. "Well I'm glad that I'm near Diablo! After all, you never know, " she said softly, sliding closer to Kevin, who had settled down in the straw.

"Hey, are you two in here?" Chester's voice came from somewhere in the stable. Quickly the two kids stood up and waved to the likeable groom.

"I just wanted to tell you that we're going to switch on the alarm system in ten minutes. Oh wait, I almost forgot something!" Chester pulled a cell phone out of his jacket pocket.

"Here! I hope you know how to work it," he grinned. "If you notice anything strange going on, call everyone! Understand? There are numbers for Mario, Jim, and me in the memory, so you can reach all of us. Keep the phone turned on, okay!?"

"Okay!"

"Well, then good night, and sleep tight till morning," he said, and then the stall door slammed shut.

"Sleep? That's a joke, right?" replied Kevin and put the phone in his pocket. "If we intended to sleep, we would have stayed in our own beds!"

Mrs. Highland stood with her arms folded behind the window of her office and stared calmly out into the night. She had turned off the light a while ago so that she could see better in the dark.

Of course, she had not missed the fact that the kids had quietly slunk from one stable to the other and had disappeared behind the doors. Eleanor had been tempted at first to order them back to their rooms, but then she decided to let them be.

She knew she wouldn't have let anyone stop her either when she was their age, if it concerned her horses. In addition, her trustworthy stable staff was with them, and that gave her an added sense of security.

"Nothing must happen," Mrs. Highland said softly to herself. "Whether the kids are in the stables or not, nothing must happen!"

Punctually at 10 o'clock, Chester switched on the alarm system. With an almost inaudible click, the windows and doors of each stable were protected from invaders.

If anyone tried to get into or out of the buildings, lights would start blinking in the local police station and a loud beeping noise would signal the need for the police to arrive at Highland Farms Estate. They would be there in only a few minutes.

Mrs. Highland took a deep breath as she regarded the blinking lights on her security system's control panel, located on her desk.

Man is such an unpredictable creature, she reflected, and then returned to stare out the window again. *We've gotten to the point where we have to protect ourselves from each other, and our animals from cruel and evil intruders who would injure them. It's inhuman!*

Eleanor Highland hunched her shoulders and, filled with an inner cold, she rubbed her arms. Suddenly she felt dead tired. But it wasn't exhaustion that made her wish for sleep. It was the helplessness she felt toward people who would get around alarm systems in order to carry out their evil plans.

She jumped, startled by the phone's ringing, and needed a moment to regain her calm.

"Yes?" she answered abruptly, and closed her eyes in annoyance when she realized who was at the other end.

"Dear Mrs. Highland, Jonathan von Branden here! We had the pleasure of meeting recently."

Pleasure is relative, thought Gwendolyn's grandmother and wearily sat down on her desk chair, feeling bothered by his call. What did this man want? She thought she had made herself perfectly clear on the subject of Garibaldi.

"What is the reason for this late call, Mr. von Branden?" she asked in a cold, bored tone.

"Well, I hope you'll excuse me, madam, for disturbing your well-deserved sleep, but the thought of your wonderful stallion just won't leave me in peace."

"As I told you, Garibaldi is – and remains – not for sale!" replied Mrs. Highland, angry about the lateness of this intrusion. "Is that the reason for your call?"

"I thought as much, that you haven't changed your mind." Von Branden laughed quietly into the telephone receiver. "And therefore, dear Mrs. Highland, I wanted to ask you if you would at least be willing to sell that very

53

noble Phoenix, your magnificent roan, who is in the stall next to Garibaldi. He seems to me to be an excellent stud."

Mrs. Highland exhaled audibly. Then she answered in an angry voice, "Couldn't you have asked that question tomorrow morning?"

"Well, I have to admit that I am a very impatient man, one who has to have his plans realized at once. Rest assured that a simple yes from you would make me the happiest man on earth, even though Phoenix doesn't measure up to the qualities of Garibaldi."

What a load of rubbish! thought Eleanor Highland. Then she said, "Very well, Mr. von Branden, if you are interested in my beautiful roan, then come over tomorrow morning, please. I think we will be able to come to an agreement about Phoenix."

Von Branden suppressed a happy outburst. "Thank you, dear lady, and allow me to say that if I were in your place, I would never give up Garibaldi either."

"Good night, Mr. von Branden." Mrs. Highland ended the conversation abruptly.

"I also wish you a good night, Mrs. Highland," replied the man before he heard the click on the line. Mrs. Highland had hung up.

Insensitive boor! she thought, getting up again and going back to her vigil at the window.

Eleanor Highland would have preferred to spend the entire night standing there in order to watch over her horses, but she knew that wasn't a good idea. Tomorrow was a new day with new responsibilities and she would need her strength.

So she sighed deeply, tore herself away from the window

with a heavy heart, and left her office, her shoulders hunched with worry and her feet dragging slowly.

When Hudson, the butler, who had run into his employer in the hallway and wished her a good night, joined his girlfriend, Martha, in the little sitting room off the kitchen, he whispered, "She looks like she's aged ten years at least. That's not a good sign."

Chapter 4

Howard Algrin was still sitting in his office at the police station, although he could have gone home hours ago. Exhausted, he stared at the huge pile of files that lay scattered on the desk in front of him, illuminated by the sparse light of his desk lamp.

He kept going over the reports of the horse butcher who had been terrorizing animals and their owners in the area for some time.

Was there really only one man involved? he wondered, but then he shook his head firmly. No. One person couldn't possibly have done so much harm! Weary, he glanced at the other paperwork that had landed on his desk; reports of several burglaries.

For a long moment, he closed his eyes and stretched out his limbs. *A bed,* he thought, as he yawned loudly. *My kingdom for a bed!*

"Coffee, Howard?" Sam French came through the open door and held up a coffee pot and mug invitingly.

"Real coffee or instant?" asked Algrin, rubbing his eyes.

"At this hour of the night, it's real, of course!"

"Than pour me some, and fill it to the brim! Black, no milk or sugar. I need all the help I can get tonight."

"Coming right up, boss!" Sam filled the mug and put it down on the desk in front of his colleague.

Noticing the open files, he asked, "You still trying to make some sense out of those horse mutilations?"

Algrin shrugged his shoulders. "I don't know," he said, more to himself than to Sam. "I've looked through these files again and again, and I know that something's not right, but I just can't figure out what it is."

At that moment the telephone rang.

"Who can that be at this time of night? Is Katie still at the main desk?" Without waiting for Sam's answer, Howard picked up the receiver.

"Algrin speaking," he said and suppressed another yawn. Then, suddenly, he was wide awake. "What did you say? Say that again!"

Sam sat on the edge of the desk and tried to read Algrin's eyes, staring at him questioningly.

"What's wrong?" He mouthed the words, but Algrin just gestured for him to be quiet.

"Tell them we'll be right there! We're on our way!" Very quickly the police Sheriff slammed down the receiver and got up.

"Alarm from the Hamilton Exhibition Stables. One of the riders observed a suspicious, darkly clothed man holding a long thin object behaving strangely between the stalls. Get me Singer, Donnelly, and Panachek – immediately!" he ordered.

"Singer is on vacation, Donnelly has already gone home, and Panachek –"

"How come Singer is on vacation again? Never mind! Call Donnelly. Tell him to get out of his cozy chair and hurry over to the Hamilton Stables." Then walking to the opened door of his office, Algrin yelled into the hallway, "Panachek! Panachek! ... Duty!" and less than two minutes later both men were running to their vehicles.

*

"Everything seems quiet," Mac whispered tonelessly as he and Cal approached the property walls surrounding the estate. They had left their car with an old inconspicuous horse trailer attached to it in the nearby woods.

"At this time of night, Mrs. Highland won't be dancing a tango in the corridors of the stables!" Cal replied quietly but in his usual nasty tone of voice. "We'll wait another thirty minutes before we attack," decided Cal and looked at his illuminated watch. "If we haven't heard or seen anyone by then, we'll go in – that is, if your wire contraption works!"

Mac's pride in his electronic capabilities was hurt, and he decided that this was the last time he was going to work with Cal Tribble. He didn't need someone always belittling him like that.

Insulted, Mac crouched behind the thick bush near the riding ring that was located behind the mares' stable.

"You didn't forget to bring the plan, did you?" asked Cal suddenly.

"No!"

"Well, I wouldn't put it past you!" grumbled Cal quietly to himself.

"What makes you think you can talk to me like that?" Mac could hardly contain his anger toward his accomplice.

Cal grinned evilly. "You don't really want to hear the answer to that, do you?" he replied, when at that moment he felt his cell phone vibrate and then ring, which meant he had a text message.

Mac, who was about to get up in a rage, took a deep breath and crouched down again. "Can't you turn that darned thing off when we're out at night? I'm sure your girlfriend can wait until you're back!" snarled Mac, furious.

"Shut up!" growled Cal, and he glanced at the illuminated display on his cell phone.

Everything okay with you? Are you there? Definitely don't start too early! The grooms inspect the stalls at 10:30. Greetings, X

"He must think we're complete idiots," complained Cal, and he turned his cell phone off without answering the message.

"As though we had the time to talk to him right now! 'Stall inspection,' ridiculous! That was a long time ago. He should just let us do our work and not bother us! The only thing that interests me is the money."

Just to be on the safe side, Cal glanced at his watch again, which showed exactly 11:15. "He must have pressed the wrong number when he was messaging. The lights in the stables went out at ten thirty."

Mac suppressed his comments and stared fixedly at the individual buildings. Somewhere over there was a switch for the alarm system, which he intended to turn off by a complicated remote-control device he had constructed.

"Contraption!" Mac ground his teeth in rage over Cal's term for his ingenious device. His hands clamped around the little box in his jacket pocket. He knew that the remote control would work, but he was still terribly nervous.

"Come on," snapped Cal. "If we wait much longer, the sun will come up!"

"But I was thinking –" began Mac, but as usual, Cal Tribble didn't let him finish.

"Let me do the thinking," he growled, and crouching, he sprinted over to the main house. He waited in the darkness behind the large veranda for his accomplice.

"Where do we have to go?" he asked when Mac finally stood next to him.

"Over there. In that long building."

"Oh, yeah, I remember. That's where they took that stallion yesterday. Good, let's go! Switch that thing off so we can start. I'll be glad when it's all over and the stallion is in the trailer."

Mac nodded and realized that this was the first thing today that he and Cal agreed on.

*

Gwendolyn paced nervously back and forth in the stallions' stable. Mario, who had run out of stories with which to distract her, rolled his eyes in annoyance.

"For goodness' sake, Gwen, sit down and try to get some sleep! You're going to make Garibaldi jumpy if you keep on pacing like that! Remember, he needs his sleep, too. After all, he has work to do tomorrow. The mares –"

"Oh, Mario, what should I do? I can't sleep! When I think that somewhere out there a crazy person is running around, who –"

"Gwen! That's enough. You're driving yourself crazy! You know we have an alarm system, and it works perfectly! Even a mouse couldn't get in without being seen!" said Mario, grasping Gwendolyn by her arms.

"Are you sure?" The girl looked at him doubtfully.

"Yes! Now lie down and go to sleep! I promise to wake you if anything unusual happens here. Honest!"

Gwendolyn sighed deeply and stroked the sleepy-looking Garibaldi lovingly across his forelock. "Okay. To be honest, I'm really tired, but –"

"No buts! Here ... here's a blanket, now go to sleep. Don't worry, I'll stay on guard." Mario's voice calmed her down, and finally Gwendolyn stretched out on the straw.

"I'm only going to sleep for five minutes, then I'll be fine," she said. "... not enough caffeine ..." was the last thing the groom understood of her mumbling before Gwendolyn dozed off. However, very soon after, she jerked awake and got to her feet again.

"I'm too nervous to sleep," she mumbled and staggered over to the feed bins to eat one of Martha's sweet rolls.

*

Lillian was having a similar time in the yearlings' stable. Jim turned out to be pretty quiet, so she really didn't have anyone to talk with. And the more she stared into the

61

darkness, the sleepier she became. The monotonous sound of the young horses chewing lulled her into a doze. By comparison, Cathy, in the mares' stable, was wide awake, fascinated by Chester's anecdotes.

*

Ricki and Kevin sat very close together, leaning against the side of the stall, wrapped in a heavy horse blanket to ward off the chilly night air. They, too, were dead tired.

"I'm freezing," shivered Ricki and snuggled up closer to Kevin, who was tying hard to keep his eyes open.

"It would be warmer in bed about now," he whispered back. "Maybe we should move around a little bit."

"Jogging down the corridor, you mean?" asked Ricki, rubbing her thighs and upper arms to warm them.

"No, not jogging, but maybe a few exercises so that we get our circulation going."

Ricki looked at Kevin doubtfully. "And you think that will help?"

"Maybe."

"Okay, maybe a few stretches!" Ricki got up with a soft groan. "Ow, everything hurts!"

"And my feet are numb and my rear end is asleep," replied Kevin, making a face. "That's a weird feeling! And now I have to go to the bathroom. I guess I drank too much water." Awkwardly, he stood up, too, and left the stall.

"I'll be right back," he said, and realized that he could have fallen asleep standing up.

Ricki stayed in the stall and did a few exercises while Black Jack watched her with a puzzled glance. Meanwhile,

Kevin stumbled down the corridor toward the front door. Half asleep, he pulled back the bolt, which could be used from outside and inside, and went out into the fresh air.

Ah, that feels good, he thought, and rolled his head around while he took deep breaths. *Ricki should go outside, too. The fresh air would make her feel much better.*

After a few minutes, he returned to the corridor and went to use the bathroom.

Ricki, who had warmed up some, went over to the stall window and tried to look outside. The window, however was up so high that even on her tiptoes she could see only a faint outline of the building across the way. The only thing she could actually see was the wonderful starlit sky, which was truly a beautiful sight.

"What are you doing?" asked Kevin softly, as he came back to the stall.

Ricki pointed upward. "Look, the sky is so beautiful! All those stars – it's simply fantastic!" she gushed.

"The air outside is great, too!" the boy responded and hugged his girlfriend. "A few minutes outside, and my whole feeling of tiredness was blown away," he added and laughed softly.

Ricki agreed, hugging Kevin back, but then, abruptly, she pushed him away.

"Say that again!" she exploded, louder, and Kevin, taken by surprise, repeated his last sentence.

"A few minutes outside, and my whole –"

"You were in the fresh air? Outside?" Ricki stared at him in horror.

"Well, duh! You can't be in the fresh air inside," he said, mockingly.

"But –" Ricki began to tremble. "The alarm system ... Kevin, nothing happened when you went outside, how –?"

Now Kevin began to understand, and all at once his face turned pale.

"Darn! I completely forgot about the alarm system! Now what? Shouldn't the police be on their way? Gwendolyn said that they would be here in a jiffy when the alarm signal went off."

Ricki felt sick and leaned her head against her boyfriend's shoulder in fear. He had a guilty conscience. In his mind, he saw the police cars driving up to the courtyard and the furious faces of the policemen when they found out that they had responded to a false alarm.

Ricki's heart beat wildly. She stood still beside Kevin and listened closely in the darkness.

After quite a while she said, in a hoarse voice, "I don't think anybody's coming! Are you sure you weren't dreaming? I mean, maybe you weren't really outside!"

Kevin rolled his eyes. "That's ridiculous! Of course I was outside! I'm not an idiot!"

"But ... but that would mean that the alarm system isn't switched on, or that it isn't working!" the girl stammered, and, after thinking for a moment, Kevin added, "There's a third possibility."

"Which is?"

"Someone switched the alarm off."

Ricki's heart stood still. "That would mean that someone – Oh, no, Garibaldi! We have to warn the others!" Without thinking, she started to run out of the stall, but Kevin caught her just in time.

"Where are you going? Wait, we have the cell phone!"

His hands trembling, he tore the little phone out of his pants pocket and made it dial Chester's number automatically while he held it to his ear and looked at Ricki.

After a few seconds, he stared at the display in annoyance. "Darn it! We don't have any reception here!" he exclaimed and threw the cell phone into the corner in despair.

"Then we'll have to go ourselves!" Ricki said softly.

"Are you crazy? If there's someone out there who intends to hurt the horses, you can't just run outside! That's much too dangerous! He might have a knife, or an axe, or something else." Kevin talked earnestly to his girlfriend, but she just shook her head hard.

"I'm scared to death," she said. "But we can't just stand around here and wait while someone hurts Mario and Gwendolyn and takes off with Garibaldi, can we?"

Kevin didn't know how to answer to that. But he was sure that he couldn't just let Ricki run off in a panic.

For a moment, there was silence.

"Maybe I *was* dreaming," Kevin stammered, but Ricki shook her head.

"That would be the easiest solution, but I don't believe that anymore!" She shook off Kevin's hand and ran to the stall window, but hard as she tried, she couldn't see enough of the courtyard.

"What are you doing?" asked Kevin.

"I want to see outside, but I'm just not tall enough!"

"Wait!" Kevin came over and gave her a leg up. "Can you see anything now?"

"Oh, no! Let me down! Quick! There are two guys standing behind the veranda. I saw them clearly! My God, Kevin, what should we do?"

The boy stood on his toes and looked out as well.

"I don't know. I just hope they didn't see us," he mumbled. Then, after thinking it over for a moment, he said, "I could run over to the stallions' stable and try to get there before they do. If the alarm system isn't working, I could at least warn Mario and Gwendolyn."

"That won't work. I'm sure they've locked the door from the inside. You won't be able to get in, and if you knock on a window those two guys will hear you for sure," Ricki countered and hoped that Kevin wasn't going to leave her alone.

"They're gone," exclaimed the boy, who had risked another glance out the window.

"What now?" Ricki felt her knees turn to jelly.

Suddenly all of the horses raised their heads. Diablo whinnied shrilly and the others joined in.

"Oh, God, Kevin, I am so afraid!" Ricki was so upset she could barely speak. She clung tightly to Kevin's arm.

"Get down," urged Kevin and jerked her hand so that she fell to her knees, hidden behind the wall of the stall.

"What –?"

"Shh! Be quiet!" Kevin put his finger to his mouth.

Crouched down together in the corner, the two of them tried to breathe silently, although in their fear, that wasn't easy.

"Oh, no ..." groaned Ricki tonelessly as she heard the screech of the stable door. Just then she wished more than anything, that she were home in her own bed and could wake up from this nightmare.

"We have to get out of here," whispered Kevin, his mind racing feverishly. The stable door was out of the question,

66

and he couldn't remember another exit – the box windows were covered with bars, but...

Kevin pulled Ricki up from the floor. "Come with me! If we're fast, we could just make it!"

Kevin was glad that they hadn't shut the stall door. This way they could slip out without being heard and run from the stall door toward the feed-storage area.

Luckily they were wearing sneakers and the soft soles didn't make any noise.

Silently they disappeared behind the bathroom door. Kevin offered a silent prayer that the door hinge wouldn't creak when he shut the door softly and slowly turned the lock.

For one second he leaned against the door and breathed heavily.

"Come on, quick, open the window," he urged Ricki, who was shaking from head to toe and having trouble following his orders.

Finally, and with some effort, she swung herself up and sat on the windowsill. Then she climbed out and let herself drop to the ground, where she waited for Kevin, who sprang down right after her.

Luckily, the window was not high, and the grass, which grew right up to the building on this side, muffled any noise as they ran off.

After a few yards, Ricki stopped and leaned against a large birch tree.

"I think I'm going to collapse," she stammered, winded. "I ... I ... can't go on!" The fear and the excitement seemed to have robbed her of all of her strength.

"Come on, we have to keep going," urged Kevin and tried to pull her along with him, but Ricki shook her head.

"What should we do now? If we start shouting or hammering against the stable door those guys will probably be gone faster than they came here. It will take a while for Chester, Mario, and the others to understand why we're making so much noise! Oh, Kevin, what are they planning on doing in the guests' stable? Garibaldi isn't there. They have to know that, don't they? And if they leave now, then this sense of not knowing what's happening will go on forever! They have to be arrested, so that – Oh, Kevin, I'm so afraid! The horses ... Diablo ..." Ricki began to cry silently. Her nerves were completely raw.

"Stay calm," whispered Kevin. He held onto his girl-friend's hand tightly, while keeping his eyes on the guests' stable.

Ricki now turned her head back toward the stable. With frightened eyes, she tried to see if there was anything happening or at least hear something from inside. But everything seemed to be okay in there. Even the horses had calmed down again.

"What are they doing with the horses?" she asked haltingly. "Diablo and the others are never that calm when strangers are in the stalls!"

Kevin shrugged his shoulders. "Maybe it's because it's not their own stalls. Everything here is strange to them. The surroundings, the people, how can they know that those two don't belong on the estate?"

Ricki hid her face in her hands and bit her lip. She had to force herself not to cry out.

"Darn!" said Kevin softly. "We should have brought the flashlight, then we could have sent blinking warning signals to the others through the window." Then after a silent pause, he said, "You know what, let's go over to the stallions' stable anyway. If Gwendolyn and Mario aren't totally blind, they can see us through the window. I think I know which stall they've settled down in."

"But the stall windows are so high, we won't be able to get close to them from the outside," Ricki countered. Nevertheless, Kevin pulled her along with him. "It'll work somehow!"

*

The darkly clothed heavy-set man was standing on a little hill in the distance and had an infrared telescope in his hand with which he could see everything in the neighborhood clearly, even at night.

Stretched out beneath him were the paddocks of the Hamilton Exhibition Stables and the extensive training area. Large jumping areas, equestrian squares, and training circles were interspersed with wonderful riding paths.

A broad smile spread over the face of the observer, as he watched the police cars approaching the area at breakneck speed.

A glance at his watch told him that he had chosen the right time for this distraction maneuver. If Cal and Mac hadn't made any mistakes, then Garibaldi would already be on his way to the horse trailer while the police searched in vain for a suspicious person.

In his mind the man could already see the huge black stallion before him, and he knew that no other horse, either before or after Garibaldi, would mean so much to him.

Lost in his thoughts, he pushed his hands into his jacket pockets and felt the smooth, cool metal of his jackknife, the one he always had with him.

When he saw that the police had reached their goal, he lowered the telescope and went back to his car. Silently, and without lights, he let it roll forward a bit before he started the engine and drove off.

Soon he would trade his car for a horse trailer and then drive to the arranged meeting place, where Cal and Mac might already be waiting with Garibaldi.

*

"Are you sure that we're in the right stable?" Cal Tribble asked quietly. He shone his tiny blue laser light after making sure that no one was near.

"You saw where they brought him yesterday yourself," growled Mac.

"Yeah – oh, the animals are standing over there! I'm surprised that they leave their stallions unguarded here." Cal grinned wickedly. "There's a few million dollars just standing around over there! Come on, we've got to hurry before they notice something."

"At least we don't have to anaesthetize anyone this time," whispered Mac and shoved the little bottle of chloroform and the cotton balls deeper into his pocket.

"Don't put that away, the stallion may need a dose! Stop, wait, that must be him ..." Cal Tribble pulled the photo of Garibaldi out of his pocket and compared it to the black horse standing in front of him. The little white star on his forehead was somewhat hidden by his mane, but it was still visible.

70

"Look at that, the photo must be an old one, the mane is longer now. I'll have to ask the boss if that raises the value of the animal. Come on, Mac, let's go! We have to get out of here!"

Cal opened the stall door for his accomplice, and Mac entered with a lead and walked toward Diablo, who regarded him with bewilderment.

What's going on! his eyes seemed to ask, and the animal looked out at the corridor. Where was Ricki? Had she sent these two men to get him?

Willingly Diablo stepped aside and allowed Mac to fasten the lead to his halter. After that, the man quickly bound up Diablo's hooves with thick fabric, which he tied on with knots around the horse's fetlocks. Then he wrapped a strip of cloth around Diablo's muzzle to keep him from whinnying and drawing attention to himself.

"Finished," he murmured, and he led the black horse out of the corridor easily. Diablo's bound hooves made no sound.

"Come on, come on," pressed Cal Tribble. "I have a feeling that soon all hell will break loose here!" Cautiously he opened the stable door and looked around before letting Mac out with Diablo, and then he closed it carefully and ran after his accomplice.

Very quickly Mac led the black horse around the narrow side of the guests' stable – and then he ran.

Luckily he's as black as night, thought Mac, surprised that the stallion was letting him lead him away without making a fuss. He'd had completely different experiences with the other animals.

All of sudden, Mac got a bad feeling. "Cal," he whispered, "I think something's wrong!"

71

"Shut up! We've never made a mistake. Hurry up, we're almost there!"

*

The two men and the horse left the property unnoticed through a side exit in the wall, and disappeared into the darkness of the neighboring woods, as Ricki and Kevin tried desperately to get the attention of Mario or Gwendolyn.

They kept jumping up in front of the window of the stall where they thought the two were on guard, but as much as they tried, they weren't heard or seen, and everything seemed quiet and calm in the stallions' stable.

Ricki and Kevin had no way of knowing that Gwendolyn and Mario had gone into the saddle room so they could have some light in order to read the latest article about Garibaldi in the *Riding Journal*, which the groom had brought with him to pass the time.

Chapter 5

"What do you think? Are they asleep?" Kevin, breathless from jumping, bent forward, and pressed his hands against his hips.

"You know what?" panted Ricki as she peered at the guests' stable. "I don't care anymore. What I care about is Diablo! He's over there, and there's no telling what those two thugs are planning to do with the horses! It's only a matter of time until they realize that Garibaldi is in another stable, and if they come over here, it'll be too late anyway!"

Before Kevin could say anything to stop her, Ricki began to scream as loud as she could, "Help! Quick! Mario, Chester, Jim – the horse butchers are here! Hurry!"

Immediately lights went on in all the stables but the guests' stable.

Mario was the first to come running outside.

"For heaven's sake, what are you two doing out here? Where are they?" he shouted loudly. When Ricki pointed toward the guests' stable, he ran over there as though the devil himself were after him. Jim was right behind him, and Chester came about two minutes later. He had taken the time to try to turn on the alarm system, which had apparently failed, in order to signal the police, but nothing he tried worked. The alarm system didn't make a sound.

With a grimace on his bright-red face, he ran after his colleagues, who had already disappeared into the guests' stable.

In the meantime, the stallions' stable was lit up as well, and Ricki, Kevin, and the other kids, who had arrived, scared to death, were standing in front of the lit up stable staring in shock at the still-dark stable across the courtyard.

Ricki held Kevin's hand so tightly that her fingernails left deep impressions in his palms.

"Why is it so quiet over there?" she asked hoarsely. "Surely they can find them."

With an uneasy feeling, she started walking back to the guests' stable. "Something's wrong," she mumbled quietly to herself, and had just decided to start running when she saw the door open. She stopped short.

Tense with anticipation, she stared straight ahead, but except for Mario, Chester, and Jim, no one left the building.

The three men looked gravely at each other before Chester took a deep breath and walked directly toward Ricki.

"And? Where are they?" the girl asked. "We didn't see them come out, so they still have to be in there."

Chester shook his head.

"There's no one in there," he said softly and looked for help to his colleagues, who were standing behind him, probably on purpose.

You guys are no help, thought Chester, and turned back to Ricki.

"Diablo is gone!" he said in a raw, hoarse voice. Instantly, he regretted his bluntness when he saw the effect the news had on Ricki. She almost collapsed from the shock.

Idiot! he thought. *You could have handled it more gently.*

"Ricki, I ... I am so sorry," he added, but the girl just stared at him in disbelief.

"It's not true! Tell me it's not true!" she screamed at the groom. Pushing him aside, she rushed into the stable, and a minute later a loud, hysterical "Noooo ..." was heard coming from inside, followed by a dead silence.

Ricki's friends ran over to Chester and the other two men. "What happened?" Lillian asked carefully. She hadn't clearly heard what Chester had said.

"The horse is gone!" explained Mario.

"Which horse?"

"Ricki's Diablo!"

Lillian, Cathy, Kevin, and Gwendolyn all turned ghostly pale and looked at each other in shock.

"That's crazy!" Gwendolyn tried to smile crookedly. "You guys ... you're joking, aren't you? You can't be serious!"

"It's no joke!" Chester said loudly. The reality of what had just happened suddenly got through to him and, asserting his position as senior groom, he took charge. "Darn it! The horse is gone and we're standing around here doing nothing! Jim, call the police! Gwendolyn, wake Mrs. Highland, and Mario, we've got to get going. Those guys can't have gotten far by now. Come on, let's go!"

Ricki, who came out of the stable door crying and stumbling, said with a voice that was almost a whisper, "I'm going with you ... I have to find Diablo ... otherwise, otherwise I'll die!"

Chester struggled with his own composure as he saw the desperate girl, but his fury toward the horse thieves grew even stronger.

"Hold on to your girlfriend so that she doesn't follow us," he said, tight-lipped, to Kevin. "I'm sure we'll get those creeps before they disappear with Diablo."

Kevin nodded and walked over to Ricki to put his arms around her, but she shook her head weakly and pushed Kevin away.

"Leave me alone." Weeping, she turned her face aside. "I was so stupid. Why didn't I stay inside the stable? Why didn't I watch to see which direction they went with him? Why did we both run over to the stallions' stable instead of just one of us, leaving the other to watch and see what happened? ... My God, Diablo! But why did they take Diablo? Why him? I think ... I'm going ... crazy ... "

Ricki felt as if she was about to faint. "I ... want ... to go ... home ..." she cried, and she spun around abruptly to run back to the main house when she crashed into Mrs. Highland, who had been woken by all the commotion and came running outside in her nightgown and bathrobe. She'd run into Jim, who was on his way to call the police. Jim stopped long enough to give her a sketchy idea of what had happened.

Now she held on to Ricki tightly and hugged her.

"Don't worry about your horse," she tried to comfort the girl, and stoked her head. "Believe me, they won't get far. You'll have your Diablo back quicker than you think. They won't do anything to him. *At least not as long as they think he is Garibaldi*, a worried Mrs. Highland added to herself. She was absolutely sure that the thieves had made a disastrous

76

mistake. They had confused the two horses and taken Diablo instead of the stallion. But how would they react when they figured out that they had kidnapped an animal that was entirely worthless for breeding purposes?

"But what if they aren't just horse thieves? What if they're the horse butchers ... then ... oh my God! ..." The idea that Diablo could be injured or killed almost drove Ricki insane.

"Before we trample all over the area and destroy any possible evidence, let's all go – quickly but carefully – into the house and wait for the police," commanded Mrs. Highland in a firm, don't-argue-with-me voice, pushing Ricki forward.

"Gwendolyn, please ask Martha to make us a pot of strong coffee. We could all use that. Then ask Hudson and William to come immediately to the parlor. I have to know right away if either of them noticed anything. After all, their bedroom windows face the guests' stable! Jim, call our alarm company rep immediately! Get him out of bed and tell him to get over here right away, unless he wants me to sue him!"

Gwendolyn and Jim nodded and ran off, while Lillian, Kevin, and Cathy, with no chores assigned to them, felt out of place as they followed Mrs. Highland and Ricki to the house.

A few minutes later, they stared at Ricki with terrified expressions on their faces. Ricki seemed to shrink deeper into Mrs. Highland's padded armchair with each passing minute.

"Sit down!" Eleanor Highland ordered the young people in a tone that allowed for no contradictions. She observed the teenagers sitting in front of her with a penetrating eye.

"Which one of you had the glorious idea to spend the night in the stables?" she asked loudly and then answered her own question in the next instant. "I can imagine that it all stemmed from Gwendolyn!"

"But all of us –" Lillian tried to object, but Mrs. Highland just waved her aside.

"Do you have any idea how lucky you are that nothing happened to you? What could I have told your parents, if – My heavens, I even told you that ..."

The fact that she had noticed the kids creeping into the stables and hadn't done anything didn't seem to occur to Mrs. Highland at the moment.

"But we just wanted to take care of the horses," Ricki said, sniffing loudly. "We didn't want any of them to be stolen. But you're right, it didn't change anything. And now ... now, Diablo is gone because I just ran away, and because ... because the cell phone didn't have any reception! Ohhhhh!" Ricki fell back into the overstuffed chair, her nerves completely shot.

Kevin swallowed hard, got up, and went to sit on the arm of the chair. Tenderly he took his girlfriend's hands and began stroking them gently.

"Ricki," he said quietly to her. "Diablo is coming back for sure ... absolutely for sure!" and Ricki nodded with tears running down her cheeks.

"Of course," she whispered, but she wasn't convinced by Kevin's words. With glassy eyes, she watched Mrs. Highland, who was pacing back and forth in the room.

Where in the world is Algrin? wondered Eleanor Highland. *When you need the police, it takes them forever to get here!* However, a glance at the big grandfather clock showed her

78

that only five minutes had passed since Jim made the phone call.

Hmm, growled Mrs. Highland inwardly. *Still, they could be here already!*

*

"This is unbelievable!" complained Howard Algrin angrily as he stomped back into his office and, furious, threw his cap into the corner. "I'm ready to wring someone's neck!"

In the past few months there had been several late-night false alarms, causing him and his team to go out on the calls for nothing.

The people at the Hamilton Exhibition Stables, who he and his men had woken from a deep sleep, had no idea about any call, but they were also upset on hearing about the tip the police had received. It meant that they were being watched.

Just to be on the safe side, Algrin and his team had searched the area around the training camp, but they found nothing to indicate that a stranger or strangers had in any way harmed the animals or tampered with the equipment. After an hour and a half, Algrin finally called off the search and had returned to his office, enraged.

"What a mess!" The Sheriff hit the desk with his palm, causing the still-full cup of coffee to tip dangerously, and some coffee to spill on the pile of files on his desk.

"Just like I said, a mess!" he repeated, although this time he meant the brown splotches on his documents.

"Man, don't just stand there with that silly look on your face, hand me a paper towel," he shouted at Peter Donnelly.

Nevertheless, Peter couldn't conceal a grin. "What do I look like, a cleaning lady?" he asked good-naturedly. Algrin made a face and grabbed the roll himself.

"Today just isn't my day," he exclaimed dejectedly as he attempted to blot-dry the damp papers.

"Oh, no, not again," he groaned, as the telephone rang. "What?!" he answered grumpily without stating his name.

"Is this a false alarm again, or is it the real deal?" he asked after a while. "Okay! We're on our way! Looks like we won't get to bed at all tonight! Thanks, Katie, and by the way, Katie, go home! Yeah, sure. Good night and thank you!"

Slowly he lowered the receiver and stared at Donnelly for a moment. With a grin on his face, Peter Donnelly reached across the desk with the cap that Algrin had thrown into the corner.

"Here, Chief! This time *you're* driving! I'm sick and tired of it for today!"

"What am I, your chauffeur?" Algrin imitated his colleague with a grin before he turned serious again. "Forget about it! You're driving! And you're driving right now! A horse has been stolen from Highland Farms Estate. I imagine Eleanor Highland is beside herself!"

"Oh, terrific! That's just how I imagined this evening ending," sighed Donnelly and thought of his girlfriend at home, whom he had promised a romantic evening. "Who's going to pay for the flowers I'll need to calm Sharon down?" he asked, but Algrin had other problems.

"Get five men together, and then let's go! Maybe we'll get lucky and find the perps. After all, with a horse in tow they won't be able to just disappear! I'd love to know how those guys switched off the alarm. That system is darn near tamperproof."

*

Mac sat in the driver's seat of the rusty old Jeep and tried desperately to keep the vehicle and the horse trailer steady on the narrow stony path.

Completely focused on his driving, he stared straight ahead, while Cal Tribble put his feet up on the dashboard, closed his eyes and lazily whistled a tune.

"Can't you be quiet? Your whistling is getting on my nerves," exclaimed Mac, grinding his teeth and holding the steering wheel even tighter, as the car jumped over a pothole.

"Mac, that was really good today. If it always went this well, we could do three gigs a night!" Cal lit a cigarette and relaxed.

"Put out that stinky butt! You know I can't stand the smoke!" Mac snapped.

But Cal just laughed. "You can get out, if you don't like it," he replied, and blew a cloud of smoke directly into his accomplice's face.

Mac started to cough and could hardly keep the car under control. The trailer began to weave back and forth dangerously on the bumpy road.

Diablo whinnied nervously. He didn't understand what was happening to him, but he instinctively felt that danger threatened. In response, Diablo thundered against the wall of the trailer with his rear hooves. But the horse's poundings sounded like rocks hitting the car and trailer from the bad road underneath, and were ignored.

"Are you crazy?" Cal Tribble yelled at his driver. "If we land in a ditch, you can forget the money! The boss won't pay for an injured horse!"

But Mac was fighting the nausea caused by the cigarette smoke. "Put that thing out!" he groaned. "I have asthma, you idiot, and this smoke is killing me!"

Tribble had a smart answer ready, but after a look at the heaving Mac, he put his cigarette out. Then he put his hand into his jacket pocket and pulled out his cell phone.

Quickly he looked for a number that he had entered into the memory, and typed in a message, since he didn't want to speak to his employer over the phone:

Job completed. We are on our way to the agreed-on meeting place. Arrival probably about 1:30. – Tribble

"And bring the money," he added verbally as he switched off his cell phone.

*

"And no one in the house heard or saw anything?" asked Howard Algrin for the third time, pacing in Mrs. Highland's living room.

"Howard, you're repeating yourself!" Mrs. Highland protested a bit loudly. "You heard what they said. Hudson and Martha were fast asleep, as was my chauffeur, William, who sleeps so soundly that the house could collapse on top of him without waking him up! I didn't notice anything either. I only woke up when the shouting began outside in the yard. You know the rest!"

82

Algrin nodded and kept taking notes while his colleagues looked around in the stalls and the yard as well as the surrounding area.

"Darn it, how often do I have to tell you that we –?" Loud voices could be heard coming from the hallway in front of the living room.

"What's going on?" Mrs. Highland asked, wrinkling her brow, as the door suddenly flew open. Astonished, Eleanor Highland and the others present stared at Mario and Chester, who were being led into the room, rather aggressively, by the police officers.

"We caught these two outside the estate walls in the nearby woods. They were pretty nervous. It appears that –" one of the policemen began his report.

"It appears that you have caught the wrong men!" Mrs. Highland trumpeted, before Howard Algrin, who also knew the two men, could say anything.

"Let my two grooms go immediately! This is just un-believable!"

Confused, the two policemen looked at each other, but they didn't loosen their grip until Algrin gave the signal.

"Thanks a lot," growled Mario, and Chester added, "Now they've had time to get away entirely. We heard a car at a place where, normally, there's never any traffic at this time of night."

"Yeah?" asked Algrin, interested.

"Yeah!"

"Would you be able to locate the place again?"

"I think so," replied Chester with a look at Mario, who was shrugging his shoulders.

"Okay, you guys, please, go with my colleagues and

show them where it is so that they can begin the search from there."

"What?" Mario snarled like a wolf. "Them?"

"Mario! Please, think of Diablo!" interrupted Mrs. Highland and gestured toward Ricki.

"Fine! Let's go!"

After the four men left, Algrin turned to the teens.

"So, now I want each of you to tell me, from your own standpoint, what happened tonight," he encouraged them, and looked up gratefully at Martha, who entered carrying a tray with a big mug of strong coffee and a platter of sandwiches, which she placed on the low table in front him.

"You are my guardian angel, Martha," groaned Algrin, who was starved. He hadn't eaten anything but a hot dog since early afternoon.

"If you bring back Diablo safe and sound, you can have dinner here for the rest of your life," announced Mrs. Highland, and Algrin nodded happily with his mouth already full.

"That's a deal, Eleanor! You wouldn't believe how much this sandwich helps a starving police officer in his work! But that's enough chatter; where should we start? Kevin, tell me your version. And please, don't leave out anything. Every small detail could be important, okay?"

The boy nodded and, after a quick glance at Ricki, began to describe in detail everything that had happened that night. The Sheriff listened closely.

*

The driver of the transport vehicle was becoming more and more euphoric. While his foot pressed down on the gas pedal, he caught himself imagining Garibaldi's descendants. He was already gleefully celebrating his success. With the foal that this stallion would sire, he would make a fortune! His bank account would be filled with millions of dollars. Finally, he, who had begun as a petty pickpocket, would achieve all of his goals and desires.

Beep-beep-beeeep, shrilled his cell phone, signaling a message. He drove onto the shoulder in order to read the message Tribble had sent him.

"Wonderful," he said quietly to himself. "But that idiot could have called me!"

After glancing at the clock on the dashboard he pulled the car back onto the road, tires screeching. He was still making good time, and it looked like the two men and he would arrive at the meeting place at the same time.

After about ten miles he saw the blinking lights of a roadblock far up ahead.

Darn, he thought, *the cops are faster than I thought!* Without slowing down he turned into a small side road that wasn't blocked. Unfortunately, this road wouldn't lead him to the place he wanted to go. Police cars were searching the area thoroughly, and he realized that it wouldn't be so easy to get to the meeting place. All the main roads in the area were being watched.

We have to get out of this area as fast as possible, he decided. *We may even have to hide the animal for two or three days.*

The man drove the transporter over to the side of the road and tried to call Tribble, but Cal had his cell phone switched off and all he could get was his voice mailbox.

"You idiot, why did you turn your cell phone off?" he yelled into the little apparatus. "Careful, the police are out looking! Don't drive to our meeting place, whatever you do! Understand? I can't get there without being seen. Drive Garibaldi back to the vicinity around the estate, making a wide circle. The mill would be the best place; there are enough little buildings around there to hide the stallion. No one will think that the animal has been hidden there. They'll think that you're already far away. I'll call back tomorrow morning to give you more instructions. Good-bye!"

Frustrated and furious, he turned the vehicle around and drove toward home.

"I can only hope those two idiots know how to handle the animal! Stealing and transporting is one thing, but taking care of Garibaldi is another," he mumbled to himself.

*

"I have to go to the bathroom," Cal Tribble said to Mac. "Stop the car up ahead."

"I think I should drive as fast as possible to the meeting place," Mac replied curtly.

"What am I supposed to do, go in my pants?"

Mac grinned at him indifferently, but then he turned onto the shoulder, where Cal got out and disappeared behind the trees.

The driver's glance fell on the cell phone that had fallen out of his accomplice's jacket pocket. He grabbed it quickly, typed in his pin number and then heard the beeping that signaled a message had been stored.

Hmm, mailbox, he thought. *I don't know how to work this thing. Darn.*

"Hey, what are you doing with my cell phone? Give that back right away!"

"You have a message. It's from the boss, for sure!" Mac informed him. Cal pressed a number lazily and then listened attentively.

"You idiot!" it screamed into his ear, making him jump. It was as though his employer were on the phone now.

After a few seconds he switched off the cell phone and sat down on the passenger seat with his lips pressed together.

"And? What did he want?" asked Mac, curious, as he restarted the engine.

"Turn around!" yelled Tribble.

"What?" Mac's eyes narrowed to slits.

"Can't you hear? I said, turn around! We're driving back. The boss wants us to hide this stupid animal at the old mill. Cops are everywhere, and he can't get to the meeting place."

"You're not serious, are you? I've been driving around for more than an hour, and now I'm supposed to drive the whole way back? Oh, no! Not me!" Mac turned off the engine again and crossed his arms. He refused to drive even one more yard.

"I guess we're supposed to baby-sit this old horse, too? We're being paid for kidnapping and transporting the animal to the meeting place, not for being baby-sitters! I won't do it!"

"I already told you, you can quit if you want to!" sneered Tribble, although for once, he shared Mac's opinion. But all this complaining didn't change anything. If they wanted their share of the money for this valuable stallion, they would have to obey the boss's orders, whether they liked it or not.

Chapter 6

Ricki slept fitfully. She kept dreaming of Diablo, trapped in a tight stall, bucking and trying desperately to free himself, and yet helpless against the hard boards that pressed painfully against his flanks, leaving bleeding patches where they rubbed against his coat.

The girl woke up covered in sweat and remained in bed a while, staring at the white ceiling and thinking about what had happened during the night.

Please God, she thought, close to tears. *Don't let anything happen to Diablo! I don't know what I'd do if he disappeared forever! What kind of monster does things like this?*

Someone knocked softly on the door.

"Ricki? Ricki, are you awake?" Gwendolyn opened the door a little, and cautiously looked in the room.

"Come in," said Ricki, sighing deeply as she slowly propped herself up.

"How are you? Everything okay?" Gwendolyn was really worried about her friend, and of course Ricki realized that, but the question, whether everything was okay ...

"Nothing is okay! Is there any news? Have they found Diablo? Has Algrin called in? Is the ..."

"Ricki, be patient. It's only six-thirty. Even police Sheriffs have to sleep sometime, don't they?" Gwendolyn tried to make her tone gentle, but even this was too much for Ricki.

"Then why did you come? Why aren't you sleeping? After all, your horses are still safe in their stalls. You don't have anything to worry about, do you?"

Gwendolyn swallowed hard. She could easily understand her friend's reaction. She would have reacted in the same way if it had been Garibaldi instead of Diablo that was missing.

"Do you want something to eat? Martha made some fresh cinnamon rolls a half hour ago."

"I'm not hungry! Leave me alone!"

"But – "

"Leave me alone! Just leave, period!" Ricki allowed herself to sink back down on the soft pillow and turn her face to the wall.

Now it was Gwendolyn who got mad. "If you keep on feeling sorry for yourself, you aren't helping Diablo! Don't be so nasty. It's not my fault that your horse was stolen. I thought maybe you'd be interested in riding around the area with us this morning. Maybe we can find something that will tell us where Diablo might be. But if you'd rather stay in bed and whine, then we'll just go without you! If, however, you should decide that you want to help look for your horse, you'll find us in the kitchen! We're hungry, even if you aren't! 'Bye, Ricki!"

With these words, Gwendolyn rushed out of the room in a fury. Once the door was closed, however, she glanced sadly at Lillian, Cathy, and Kevin.

"I have no idea if she'll come with us," she said softly as the friends walked silently to the kitchen. To be honest, they had lost their appetites, too. They were all too worried about Diablo.

Ricki, who had acted as though she hadn't even heard Gwendolyn's accusations, grabbed her pillow and threw it as hard as she could at the door through which her friend had disappeared. She was mad at herself. She knew she had been unfair to Gwen, who had just wanted to help.

"Stupid ninny!" Ricki said to herself and slowly got out of bed. Still a little stiff, she padded over to the vanity sink and stared into the mirror.

"You can whine all you want, Ricki Sulai," she scolded herself. "If Diablo means as much to you as you say he does, then get going and start looking for him!" Ricki stuck her tongue out at herself angrily and splashed the mirror with a handful of water so that her image was distorted.

"Serves you right!" she said softly. She brushed her teeth, then combed her hair and tied it up in a ponytail. She dressed quickly and hurried out of her room.

I hope the others are still here, she thought as she headed toward the kitchen. Just as she was about to open the door, she heard Gwendolyn say, "I have no idea where we should begin looking, but Mario said last night that the guys had hidden their trailer in the woods and probably loaded Diablo into it there."

"Darn it! If they had a trailer with them they could be anywhere. Can someone tell me how we're supposed to find Diablo? We don't have a clue!" Kevin said what everyone else had been thinking.

"That's true," responded Gwendolyn. "But don't you think it would help Ricki more if she knew she was doing something useful to help find her horse rather than just sitting around here and letting herself think all these negative thoughts?"

"Absolutely," replied Lillian. "But I don't know what's helpful, really, about riding around here looking for Diablo, when we know that he isn't anywhere near here."

"Oh, come on, that's not what this is about!" Cathy swallowed a too-big piece of her cinnamon roll and started to have a coughing fit. When she got her breath back, she said, "Ricki has to keep herself occupied, otherwise she'll go crazy worrying about Diablo! Would you guys react any differently? I think if someone stole Rashid, you could take me straight to the loony bin."

Her friends nodded. No one envied Ricki's situation. If only they knew where to search for Diablo.

Ricki swallowed hard and then pushed open the swinging door and went into the kitchen.

"Hey," she said softly and tried to smile before going over to Gwendolyn. "Gwen, I'm sorry about what I said before."

Gwendolyn stood up and wrapped her arms around her. "That's okay," she replied "So, you're coming with us?" she asked, easing Ricki down onto a chair, while Kevin handed her a sweet roll and a glass of juice.

"I just overheard your conversation," she said, and looked around at them in dismay.

"Oh," exclaimed Lillian, a little red in the face. "Did you ... I mean, did you hear everything?"

Ricki nodded. "Yeah, I heard everything, but you're only half right. I don't want to be distracted from the situation itself, and if I go riding, then it's only because I think I have a tiny chance of finding Diablo. Even though it probably won't happen."

"Then let's get going," decided Gwendolyn. "You know what they say about the early bird catching the worm!"

"Well, if that's true, then we'd better hurry," said Ricki. "Which horse can I ride?"

Gwendolyn licked the sugar glaze from her fingers and thought it over for a moment.

"Hmm, I'd lend you Black Jack, but he only lets me ride him. Maybe ... yeah, perfect – you can have Aladdin! He's great, and you'll like him!"

"Which one is he?" Ricki asked, her curiosity aroused.

"The black sorrel with the wide star. You must have seen him on the paddock."

Ricki thought about it, but couldn't remember seeing the gelding.

"Good, then let's hurry up with breakfast," she urged her friends. "I can't stand this waiting around, doing nothing!" She wolfed down the cinnamon roll and juice and then slid around on her chair impatiently until her friends had finished theirs.

*

Sheriff Algrin had taken only a two-hour sleep break on the couch in his office, and since early that morning had been sitting at his desk, reading through all the documents concerning the horse butchers.

He had examined everything very carefully once again, only this time he was suddenly struck by something that all of the cases had in common; every time something had occurred at the horse farms, there had been a call made to the local police station beforehand, a call that had led the police on a wild goose chase.

"Good grief, I am such an idiot!" he exclaimed, striking his forehead with his hand.

He got up abruptly and went downstairs to the reception area, where he began to look in the archives for all the tapes of the calls that had come in concerning this case. All calls that caused the police to intervene were automatically taped. Algrin suddenly had an idea.

He raced back up to his office with his arms full of tapes and then began to compare them.

He kept replaying the tape of the mysterious man who reported a problem last night at the Hamilton Stables to Katie, and then he listened to the other tapes that had directed them to false leads.

After about half an hour, Algrin slapped his thigh and grinned at the tape recorder as though it were his best friend. The anonymous calls all seemed to be made by the same man.

"Howard, now you have made some progress!" he announced to himself, and packed the tape from last evening and the portable tape recorder into a duffel bag and quickly left his office.

"Eleanor, I hope you're up," he smiled as he started the engine of his car and drove off in the direction of the stud farm.

*

Cal Tribble had threatened Mac with exposing his alarm-system blocking device to the police if he didn't drive the horse back to the mill.

"You're a lousy rat," was the last thing that Mac had said to his accomplice after turning the vehicle around.

He'd been sitting behind the wheel for almost three hours without a break, and all the while looking for side roads so as to avoid running straight into the arms of the police. Now he turned off into the narrow lane that led to the abandoned mill. Mac sweated buckets until he finally reached the building. The narrow path wasn't really made for traffic, so he had to concentrate on keeping the car and the horse trailer from sliding into the ditches on either side.

When they finally arrived, Mac, who was exhausted, ignored Cal's instructions to unload the horse and stayed seated in protest. His accomplice had to unload the horse from the small horse trailer himself. He didn't have any other choice.

Diablo was upset by the long drive and laid his ears back aggressively as Cal appeared beside him to untie the ropes.

"Don't you dare bite me, you stupid beast!" growled the man angrily, and Diablo sensed that he would have to be careful around this man.

Cautiously the animal took one backward step after another down the loading ramp and snorted when he finally had firm ground under his hooves. He whinnied loudly into the night and listened closely to see if he could hear Ricki's voice somewhere. But all around him was silence.

"Quiet!" yelled Cal and pulled harshly on his lead while he felt around with his other hand to find the piece of cloth that Diablo had shaken off his muzzle.

"You're not going to give us away!" Cal said in a gruff whisper and then tied the black horse's muzzle shut again with the cloth.

Diablo heard the water rush by in the stream a few yards away and he felt a great thirst, but this man wouldn't let him drink.

"Come on, let's go!" he ordered Diablo, and he pulled the unwilling black horse behind him roughly. A few minutes later he tied him to a heavy rusted iron stand in the old shed directly behind the mill.

"Oh, man, I will be so glad to get rid of you!" groaned Cal, wiping the sweat from his brow. He had never been able to understand how some people could find these animals so wonderful.

"They're all crazy," he mumbled to himself, while he walked over to the horse trailer, lifted the loading ramp and slammed it shut.

Afterward he opened the door on the driver's side and shook his accomplice, who had fallen asleep from his exertions.

"Hey, Mac! Wake up! You have to drive the car behind the shed! Hey! Hey!"

Mac started as he woke up. "Just leave me alone!" he yawned. "I'm not driving one foot farther!"

"Well, if that's what you want – that when it gets light, someone might see us – then leave the car here!"

The driver made a fist. He was so sick and tired of Cal Tribble. Then he suddenly had an idea that made him very happy.

What would he do if I just drove away? he asked himself, and in the next instant he decided to do just that. *Tribble could just get lost!* And the dough? *Ah, who needs it,* he thought. *The last few robberies brought in enough.* The thought of leaving this annoying man here alone made him laugh. This would be a way of paying him back for all the mean things he had done.

Slowly he put his hand on the key and turned the engine on.

"All right, finally!" Cal stepped back with a grin as Mac stepped on the gas.

The engine roared, the tires spun before they got traction, and Mac, together with the trailer, drove off across the field next to them.

Cal stared in bewilderment at the receding taillights.

"Is he crazy?" he said aloud to himself before yelling after Mac, "You stupid idiot! Come back here immediately!" But his former accomplice just waved to him out of the window and disappeared into the darkness.

*

It was daybreak, and Cal Tribble, in a very bad mood, was pacing back and forth in the old shed. He glanced evilly at the horse he believed was Garibaldi.

"What am I going to do with you, you stupid beast? If only the old man would get here already! This thing is getting to be too hot to handle and I can't even drive away! And I'm hungry! Oh, that Mac, I could ..."

Diablo glanced at the angry man and tried to kick him as he walked past. The horse could sense that this human was an enemy and had decided not to let him come near. Although, if he would bring him a bucket of water or an armful of hay ... or if he would take off that unpleasant rag that was beginning to dig into the flesh above his nostrils ...

*

The teenagers had saddled their horses quickly and were already on their way. With Aladdin, Ricki had a wonderful riding horse that reacted to every gesture and touch just as Diablo did. But she couldn't take any pleasure in the ride. Her every thought was of her lost horse.

"What do you think about riding to the place where they loaded Diablo into the trailer?" Ricki asked.

Gwendolyn shook her head. "No, we'll just be in the way. Granny asked me not to bother the police at their work."

"If only we had another clue," Ricki said for the fifth time, unaware that she kept repeating herself.

"Ricki," said Gwendolyn gently, "we're doing the best we can to search all around this area. I know every nook and cranny, and we won't leave any of them out, I promise you that! But please, don't expect to find something the thieves left behind every five minutes. They're professionals and they know exactly what they're doing."

Ricki sighed. "You're right. Excuse me, please, if I get on your nerves, but –"

"Don't worry about it!" Kevin nodded at her with sympathy. "We understand – you don't have to explain anything!"

"Good ... Thanks for all your help."

"I think first we should ride over to the cliffs where Sunshine gave birth to her foal. There are so many hidden places between the boulders where a horse could be hidden," suggested Gwendolyn. "Of course, it will take quite a while

97

to search the whole area, since we can only do it on foot. This time the horses will stay away from the cliffs."

Gwendolyn looked at the kids seriously, and they nodded vigorously in agreement as they recalled their last visit to the stud farm, and all the excitement caused by Sunshine and Diablo.

"Okay, and then what?" Lillian stared at Black Jack's rider, curious about what she would suggest next. "Where are we going to look?"

Gwendolyn thought it over quickly. "We could go on to the ruins, although I doubt they'd take him there. That's pretty close to the main road. There'd be a high risk of their being seen by the police, and those guys, whatever else they may be, aren't stupid. Another possibility would be to ride in the direction of the old mill. There are all kinds of hiding places there, old sheds, barns, thick bushes, and little cabins that are rented to hikers during the summer season. But at the moment they're all empty."

"How come? Isn't it still summer?" Cathy asked in surprise.

"Maybe they're empty because the city wants to renovate them."

"But there must be other places where Diablo could be hidden?"

"Lots," responded Gwendolyn, with a note of resignation in her voice as she glanced at Ricki.

"Well, maybe we'll get lucky at one of the places you already mentioned," Cathy said.

"Luck, yeah, we need some of that. In fact we need a ton of it," groaned Ricki. "Say, Gwen, the cliffs are pretty far away, and the old ruins are too. Wouldn't it be better to

98

check out the old mill first and maybe the cabins? That way, at least we'll have examined one place, instead of using up half a day riding aimlessly through the area."

"Hmm, maybe you're right," answered Gwendolyn. "Maybe William can even drive us there. That would save us a lot of time."

"Well, I think we've already gone half the distance to the cliffs. It would be idiotic to turn around now," volunteered Kevin. "Anyway, I don't think Diablo is near the old mill – that's much too close to the farm." He shook his head. "No, Diablo is definitely far away from here. Sorry, Ricki, but we have to consider all possibilities, even when it hurts."

Ricki nodded and tried not to cry at her boyfriend's words.

"Okay," she said softly. "Then let's go to the cliffs first. Then later maybe we'll search the mill, okay?" She looked at Gwendolyn hesitantly.

"Okay! But let's get going before it's too late!"

The horses began moving as though they had been given a signal, and shortly thereafter they were all galloping across the fields together.

Diablo, don't be afraid, thought Ricki, while the thunder of Aladdin's hoofbeats roared in her ears. *I'll find you, even if Aladdin has to carry me throughout this state and the neighboring ones. I will find you, I promise ...*

*

It was nine o'clock when Jonathan von Branden, in a good mood, called his driver.

"Martin, get the limousine out of the garage, we're going to drive over to the stud farm again." Von Branden's cordial tone relieved the anxious chauffeur. He'd been afraid that his boss was about to fire him.

"Very well," Martin answered. "I'll be there right away!"

About 9:30 Hudson announced to Eleanor Highland that Mr. von Branden had arrived. She didn't seem to be overjoyed by the idea.

"My goodness, I had forgotten about him entirely," she said and rolled her eyes. "Oh well, bring him in, but tell him that I don't have much time."

"Dear Mrs. Highland!" Von Branden oozed charm as he entered her office and gallantly kissed her hand in an old-world gesture of respect. "Please excuse my visiting so early in the morning. I thought I'd best strike while the iron is still hot, so to speak."

Bewildered, Eleanor Highland regarded her visitor. "I don't understand what you mean."

"Well, I was afraid that you might change your mind about selling Phoenix."

She got up abruptly. "Oh! Well, come with me. Perhaps you'd like to see him again before you decide to buy him," she said, and walked quickly and firmly out of her office. Never letting up on the pace, she reached the stallions' stable in no time, while von Branden had some difficulty keeping up with her.

"I didn't come here to run a marathon," he panted, a little out of breath, but Mrs. Highland just ignored his objections. She wanted to get this over with so that this Jonathan von Branden would disappear again.

"Well, we haven't even discussed the price," she said, as she headed toward Phoenix's stall.

But von Branden's glance was drawn magically to Garibaldi's

stately appearance. Just as on the previous day, he stared in awe at the magnificent horse. "Garibaldi!" he exclaimed, which produced an amused little laugh from Mrs. Highland.

"You're standing in front of the wrong stall! Garibaldi is still not for sale!"

"But – "

"No buts, Mr. von Branden! What about Phoenix? Have you lost interest in him now that you've seen Garibaldi again? If that's the case, tell me now. My time is too valuable to waste standing around here all morning," announced Mrs. Highland a bit curtly.

"Exactly, my dear. I'm just not sure anymore. I need to give it more thought," he stammered as he stared in fascination at his dream horse.

"Well, at least I now know how things stand!" Eleanor Highland rolled her eyes angrily and waited a moment before she nodded at von Branden. "Might I ask you to think about it at home?"

"Excuse me?"

"I would like you to leave now, because I have other responsibilities I have to attend to!" Mrs. Highland was perfectly clear this time.

"Oh, yes. Of course. I'll get back to you soon." Von Branden left the stalls hurriedly without saying good-bye to Mrs. Highland.

"Good-bye, sir!" murmured Eleanor Highland when she heard the roar of the limousine's engine as it pulled, too quickly, she thought, out of her driveway. *Jonathan von Branden, you are a strange man,* she said to herself as she walked back to her office. She was expecting a visit from Sheriff Algrin.

101

*

The Sheriff had been delayed. Not only had his car stalled just five miles from the precinct and had to be towed, but he'd witnessed an accident and had to return to the police station to fill out a report. It was almost noon before he arrived at the Highland estate.

*

"It would appear that you schedule your visits to coincide with meal times," grinned Mrs. Highland. "I was expecting you earlier."

"I intended to be here much earlier, but ... oh, never mind. I have some news and a few questions," he replied. "Have the young people all left?"

"They're out riding. They wanted to look for Diablo themselves," Mrs. Highland responded.

The police Sheriff wasn't at all pleased. "If there had been even a small track left, by now it's been totally trampled by the kids' horses. Couldn't you keep them home?" he asked with a trace of irritation in his voice.

"*You* try to keep someone home when she's trying to find her beloved horse! That's impossible! As a rider yourself, Howard, you should know that."

"Hmm," mumbled Algrin, as he unpacked his tape recorder and tapes and put them on Mrs. Highland's desk.

"What's this?" she asked curiously.

"Just wait! Maybe this will help us to make some progress!"

"Would you like to eat something first?"

102

"No thanks, but afterward, if possible." The Sheriff smiled at his old friend.

"I'll think about it. Are you almost finished?"

"Yep! So, Eleanor, listen closely and tell me if this voice sounds familiar to you in any way." He pressed the start button on the recorder and played back the voice of the anonymous caller from the previous evening.

Chapter 6

Ricki was completely discouraged when she came back from the morning ride with her friends. They'd searched the area around the cliffs for hours looking for Diablo, and the girl had called out to him until her throat hurt, but they saw and heard nothing of her horse.

Sadly she unsaddled Aladdin, brushed his coat listlessly, and even cleaned out his hooves. With a half smile she pushed a treat between his teeth.

"You're a sweet, sweet horse," she said softly and patted his neck before hurriedly leaving his stall. She felt as if the stall was suffocating her. She ran down the corridor and back outside into the fresh air.

Gwendolyn, Lillian, Cathy, and Kevin were just coming around the corner, so together the kids walked toward the main house.

"Let's ask Granny if she has any ideas where Diablo could be," suggested Gwendolyn. And five of them headed directly for the office.

Gwendolyn was just about to reach for the doorknob when Ricki held her back.

"Stop!"

"What's going on?"

"Shh!" said Ricki and laid her ear against the door. After a few seconds, she said, "That guy is here again!"

"What guy?" Her friends looked at her questioningly.

"That guy who was trying to talk your grandmother into selling him Garibaldi! I recognize his voice!"

"What? Just wait!" Gwendolyn pushed the door open with a bang and almost fell into her grandmother's office. Astonished, she looked at Howard Algrin, who had just turned off the tape recorder.

Eleanor Highland observed her granddaughter with an accusing look. "Well, really, Gwendolyn, what's gotten into you? Can't you knock?"

"Excuse me, please, Granny, but Ricki thought that ... well ... actually, it looks as though she made a mistake."

"But I *didn't* make a mistake! I am absolutely sure!" Ricki had appeared behind Gwendolyn and looked a little insulted.

"I don't understand a word you're saying. What are you talking about?" asked an impatient Mrs. Highland, but the Sheriff interrupted her. "What are you so sure about?" he asked, and Ricki answered quickly. "The voice that I just heard, I recognize it! Do you have that voice on the tape?"

"Yes!" The Sheriff and Mrs. Highland exchanged looks.

"Would you like to hear it again?"

Ricki nodded, and Algrin played the tape from the beginning again.

"Now it sounds completely different," reacted the girl, confused.

"That's too bad," sighed Mrs. Highland.

"Stop, I think I know why. Please, Sheriff Algrin, start the tape again, I'll be right back!" Ricki flew from the room and slammed the door behind her.

"Now!" she ordered from the hallway, and listened attentively.

"It's him!" she shouted, and stormed back into the office. "Like I said before, that's the guy who wanted to buy Garibaldi! I heard his voice just once, when he was in your office, Mrs. Highland, and I heard the conversation inadvertently from behind the door."

Algrin glanced at Mrs. Highland, who fell back into the armchair.

"She could be right," she confirmed Ricki's words slowly. "But I can't imagine that he is involved in any way with the horse slaughtering, and even less with the disappearance of Diablo. Just yesterday he offered to buy Phoenix, instead of Garibaldi, whom he would never had gotten."

"If von Branden wanted to buy your best stallion and you rejected him – that could be a motive for him to steal him!" suggested Algrin.

Mrs. Highland laughed out loud. "Von Branden? Never! That would be beneath his dignity! Anyway, he wouldn't have taken the wrong horse. He was here just this morning and, as always, he was completely fascinated by Garibaldi, and that made him unsure about buying Phoenix."

"He was here? Hmm, it would be really foolish of him to come here again after stealing from you."

"But the voice –" interrupted Ricki once again.

Algrin shrugged his shoulders. "We'll have to reexamine this again closely."

Just then the phone rang.

"Yes. Ah, Frances. I don't have any time just – What? Again? Oh, no. I'm so sorry, Frances. I'll call you back later!" Mrs. Highland hung up the receiver and slowly turned to face the others. "He's struck again. Hansen's Arabian stallion ... he's dead."

Gwendolyn screamed and Ricki felt as though the floor was beginning to slide away from under her feet.

Algrin's expression became noticeably grim. "That monster!" he exclaimed through clenched teeth, as he hastily packed away his equipment into the duffel bag.

"I promise you, Eleanor, I'll get that ... that ..."

"That monster!" Mrs. Highland finished his sentence. She was visibly upset.

"I'll find him, even if I have to spend the rest of my life looking for him," said Algrin, grabbing his duffel bag. Just then his glance fell on Ricki, who had collapsed in her chair. "And your horse, too!" he added with determination.

"That would be great," answered Ricki softly, but her hope of seeing Diablo safe and happy began to disintegrate.

"I'm going back to the station to look through all the information we have on this latest incident. Then I'm going to go see this von Branden guy, and then I'll check to see if my colleagues have found any trace of Diablo. I'm sorry that I can't accept your invitation to lunch, Eleanor," he added with a sigh, but his face held a trace of schoolboy charm and humor. "I'll take a rain check, if I may."

*

Cal Tribble had turned on his cell phone hours ago and waited impatiently for a call from his boss, but the phone remained silent. Every few minutes the man stared at the display; finally he threw the phone into the corner of the shed in exasperation.

"Great, Tribble," he scolded himself. "Really great! Now what are you going to do in this godforsaken place without a car?" Furious, he sat down a safe distance from Diablo and stared at him pensively.

"Listen, Garibaldi," he threatened the black horse, raising his fist, "I can tell you one thing; if anything goes wrong, I will make you into a gelding myself. That I promise you!"

Diablo laid back his ears menacingly and, with his front hoof, fiercely kicked the iron railing to which he was tied.

"Stop making all that noise," growled Tribble, looking at the horse again. *Pretty strong, these stallions,* he thought, but then he stopped short.

"Noooo!" He bent down and squinted his eyes in an effort to see more clearly. Then he just fell over backward.

"No! No! No!" he shouted, and then he began to laugh insanely. "Cal Tribble, you stole a gelding! How can that be possible?" After he calmed down some, he wiped his sweaty brow with his hand and sat up.

"The boss will kill me," he concluded. He knew he had to get out of there right away. He might as well forget about the money – and it was all the fault of this darn Garibaldi lookalike!

He got to his feet, bent down to pick up his cell phone, and raced out of the shed. Before he locked the door carefully, he called to Diablo, "Bye, you stupid nag! Maybe you'll be lucky and somebody will find you! But I wouldn't count on it. You've cheated me out of a lot of money – as far as I'm concerned you can die here!" Cal Tribble ran off chuckling to himself. At least now he had one less worry.

*

"Do you think that von Branden had something to do with Diablo's disappearance?" Ricki asked Mrs. Highland as they were having lunch together.

"I can't imagine that myself," answered Mrs. Highland slowly, looking at the girl across from her. "But I am sure that the thief, whoever he is, has mistaken his identity. Poor Diablo just happens to look like Garibaldi, otherwise I feel sure none of this would have happened." She paused for a moment and then asked, "You love your horse very much, don't you?"

Ricki nodded. "Diablo means everything to me!" she answered after a short pause. Then, as if a dam burst inside her, she began to talk about her black horse. Everything she had ever experienced with him just flowed out of her in vivid detail, as though it had just happened.

Mrs. Highland listened closely and silently, and looked into Ricki's shining eyes as the girl talked about Diablo. Even Ricki's friends, who had experienced most of it with her, put down their silverware and listened to her relate their amazing adventures.

When Ricki finished she lowered her eyes and stared down at the table. "I miss him so much!" she exclaimed, and pushed her plate aside with a desperate gesture that knocked over the water glass standing next to it, spilling the contents onto the tablecloth. Ricki's lips trembled and a tear rolled down her cheek. "Diablo ..." The girl hid her face in her arms and sobbed pitifully.

Awkwardly, Kevin put his hand on her shoulder, but Ricki didn't seem to notice it. The most horrible thoughts raced through her brain and she felt that her fears for Diablo would drive her crazy.

"Come on, Ricki, let's go outside for a bit," Kevin suggested. He too felt sick seeing how much his Ricki was suffering. If only he knew how to help her! But he couldn't produce Diablo magically.

The girl brushed aside her boyfriend's hand, jumped up from her chair, and ran out of the dining room. Kevin wanted to run after her, but Mrs. Highland held him back.

"Let her go, Kevin," she said and pointed at his chair. "Sit down. You can't help her at the moment. No one can. It's her sadness, and, as brutal as it may sound, she will have to overcome it by herself. She needs time to get her thoughts in order. Just leave her alone for a while; that's the best thing you can do for her."

"I don't know," said Kevin doubtfully, and he kept looking at the door through which Ricki had disappeared.

"But *I* know! Believe me, I know what I'm talking about," stated Mrs. Highland with authority "But let's not talk about that. What are you all going to do this afternoon? Are you going out riding again?"

"I don't know, Granny, but I don't think so. Ricki was so frustrated that we didn't find Diablo among the cliffs. I'm not sure she could stand it if we went out again today for nothing. Maybe I could talk her into going to the movies," suggested Gwendolyn.

"Well, at least that would distract her a little." Eleanor Highland pressed her napkin against her mouth and patted her lips, and then got up to go. "Don't let me disturb you young people. Finish – enjoy your lunch. I have work to do," she smiled and left the kids alone with their worries.

"Algrin, Algrin, now's the time to show us what you can do. Bring that horse back before this girl goes completely crazy!" she mumbled to herself from her office window as she watched Ricki leaning against the paddock fence and observing her friends' horses longingly.

Briefly, Eleanor considered phoning her friend Carlotta, but she decided against it. No need to worry her with this just now. There'd be time for a conversation with her later, once the whole situation became clearer.

*

Diablo didn't understand what was happening. Lonely and incapable of making his situation known by whinnying, he stood in the dilapidated shed and tried to free himself from the rope. Tribble, however, had tied several knots on top of each other so that the individual loops just kept getting tighter the more he pulled on the rope.

Gradually the animal became impatient and anxious. Furiously he pulled on the rope with all of his strength, but it didn't budge an inch. Instead, the heavy iron railing broke off the mounting on the floor and tipped over toward Diablo.

The black horse tried to save himself from the danger by moving aside, but the short rope prevented him from doing so. The railing hit Diablo's head hard and, dazed from the blow, the horse went down. The short rope got caught in

111

the fallen railing so that he couldn't move his head more than a few inches to the side.

Frightened, Diablo opened his eyes so wide that the whites became visible. His body was covered in sweat and he was breathing heavily as he came to. The cloth around his muzzle had slid a little and was covering his nostrils so that he couldn't get enough air.

Nevertheless, gathering all of his strength, Diablo tried to get up, but the rope held him to the floor. Panicky, the black horse kicked in all directions. In the hope of finding something to hold on to, he kicked with his front legs against the iron railing lying partly on top of his head and neck, but the hoof got caught between the bars and forced him to give up.

He remained lying down, and a strange calm swept over him. An endlessly sad expression came into his wonderful eyes and it was becoming harder and harder for him to breathe.

Where in the world was Ricki? He had always been able to rely on her, and she'd always been there for him when he needed help.

Exhausted, Diablo closed his eyes and listened to the refreshing stream gurgling outside in front of the mill, so near and yet impossible to reach.

*

Ricki ran back and forth nervously between the paddocks. She was tenser than she had ever been, and every two minutes she glanced at her watch, but time seemed to be standing still today.

"Hi, still no news about Diablo?" asked Chester sympathetically as he walked past her on his way to the stallions' stable.

Ricki shook her head. "Unfortunately, no."

"Come with me, girl. You can't do anything about it anyway. I have a great job for you. Would you like to brush Golden Star's coat? What do you think? You know that we have to get the little foals used to all the equipment, like the currycomb and the hoof pick, and I think it would be the perfect job for you."

Ricki looked gratefully at him. She really appreciated his trying to get her mind off her problems, but she turned him down anyway. "Chester, I can't do it right now. I'm just too upset. But tell me, is there a bike around here somewhere that I could borrow? I can't stand it anymore, just sitting around waiting and hoping. I'd like to ride around a bit, maybe ... well, you never know. Do you understand what I mean?"

Chester nodded. "Of course, I understand! You'll find Gwendolyn's bike over there in the small garage. It's green; you can't miss it. I don't think she'll mind if you take off with it."

"Thanks, Chester. And, please, if the others ask about me, I don't want them to follow me. I really want to be alone right now. Can you tell them that?" Ricki looked at the groom pleadingly.

"Of course, but don't go too far away."

"Don't worry, I'll be back soon." Ricki ran over to the garage and grabbed Gwendolyn's mountain bike.

"Where are you headed, exactly?" asked Chester as Ricki got on the bike.

"Over to the mill," yelled Ricki over her shoulder as she started pedaling furiously. *I should have thought of this much sooner,* she said to herself as the wind whipped her ponytail around her head. Something inside her told her that she had to hurry, although she didn't know why.

As she neared the mill, she thought she heard Diablo whinnying in the distance. Scared to death, she squeezed the brakes and just managed to jump off before the abrupt stop would have caused her to fall over.

Panting from all the pedaling, she listened intently in all directions and tried to control her heavy breathing, but she was surrounded by silence.

I can't possibly have made a mistake, thought Ricki, and then she shouted as loud as she could, "Diablo, where are you?"

But she got no answer.

Confused, she got back on the bike and turned onto the narrow path between the meadows that had led them to the mill the previous day. The closer she got to the old building, the more her tension mounted. Something seemed to be wrong up there.

Strange, she thought, *yesterday, this mill looked so peaceful and quiet, and today ... But maybe it's just because I'm searching for Diablo. Dear God, please help me find him.*

*

"Police district six, French speaking," Algrin's colleague answered the phone. "Hello? Hello! Say something..."

"Yes, hello!" said a muffled voice.

Oh-oh, thought Sam French. Immediately he turned on the tape recorder.

"Who is it?"

After a few seconds, the anonymous speaker continued. "The stallion is in the mill!"

"Which stallion?" asked French.

"Cal Tribble stole him!"

"What? Say that again. Hello? Hellooo!" French shook the receiver as though trying to force the conversation to continue, but Mac had already hung up.

"Well, now it's getting exciting!" French turned off the tape recorder quickly and dialed Algrin's cell phone number, but just as it began to ring, Algrin walked through the door.

"What?!" Algrin answered the ring automatically, and French, seated at his desk, had to grin.

"Hello?! French speaking. You won't believe the anonymous call I just got!"

Algrin looked at his colleague in amazement and then hung up the phone.

"What call?"

"Cal Tribble stole a stallion, and he's supposed to be in the old mill!"

"Tribble? I thought he was still in prison! When was he released? Well, it doesn't matter now. Send out an all-points bulletin on him right away. I'm sure he's still in the area. Where did the caller say the stallion was? In the old mill? Didn't Panachek search that building? That would have been the first place – Jeez, if I don't do everything myself ..."

"There's some truth to that!"

"Well, I'm going to drive over there right now. By the way, the stallion is probably a gelding, and his name is Diablo!" Algrin turned immediately and ran back to his car.

"Aha," said French. "Diablo! Why not?!" he said to himself, and went to make himself a strong cup of coffee before he began looking up the names of people known to have been Tribble's accomplices in the past. One of them might have been the anonymous caller.

*

"Eleanor, we got an anonymous tip that Diablo is in the old mill! I'm already on my way there. Tell Ricki to cross her fingers." Algrin shouted all this into the telephone, causing Mrs. Highland to hold the receiver a few inches away from her ear.

"Howard, we'll be right there! If Diablo is really in the mill, then –"

"What? I can't understand you, the connection is really bad!"

"No, no, the connection is perfect, don't shout so loud!"

"What?"

Eleanor Highland shook her head and just hung up. If Howard couldn't understand her, there was no point in continuing the conversation anyway.

Quickly she left her office and walked into the hallway.

"Gwendolyn!" Eleanor Highland's voice and urgent tone could be heard throughout the house. "Gwendolyn, where in the world are you kids?"

"For heaven's sakes, Granny, why are you shouting? Did something happen?" Mrs. Highland's granddaughter raced down the stairs and stopped short in front of her grandmother.

"Howard Algrin called. Diablo seems to be in the old mill!"

116

"What? That means Ricki was on the right track! I have to tell her immediately! Do you know where she is?" She looked at her grandmother questioningly.

"The last time I saw her, she was standing at the birch paddock, but that was quite a while ago."

"Then I'm going to go look for her right away! She can't be far." Happy at the turn of events, Gwendolyn was looking forward to telling her girlfriend the encouraging news.

"Do that! And when you find her, let me know, please. Have William drive us out to the mill."

"Okay!"

On her way outside, Gwendolyn went past Lillian, Cathy, and Kevin's rooms, and hammered on their doors.

"Come on, everybody, come with us! Sheriff Algrin may know where Diablo is!" she shouted. She had already gone through the front door when her bewildered friends met in the hallway.

"What did she say?" asked Cathy, but Kevin just shrugged.

"I have no idea, but I think it was something about Diablo!"

"What? Then let's follow her, quick!" Lillian raced off and just caught a glimpse of Gwendolyn in the front yard running up to Mario and asking him something.

"Hey, what's going on?" Lillian called to her girlfriend.

"I'm looking for Ricki! Do you have any idea where she could be?"

"Nope!"

"Darn it! Chester, Chester, have you seen Ricki?" Gwendolyn ran after the second groom, whom she had discovered behind the stallions' stable.

"She wanted to ride to the old mill on your bike," Chester informed them easily. "But she asked me to tell you all to not follow her. She said she wanted to be alone!"

"Great, but it's not going to happen. Howard Algrin called and said that Diablo may be there. William is driving us there."

"Then good luck!" Chester wished them, but Gwendolyn was already on her way back to get William.

*

"Oh, look, who do we have here?" murmured Howard Algrin behind his steering wheel, as he observed a man in dirty clothes running toward the main road and continually looking behind him as though he were being chased.

If that isn't Tribble, then I'll eat my hat, the Sheriff thought. He remembered the criminal very well. He had sent him to prison more than five years ago.

Quickly he radioed his colleagues. "I want Singer to check a stretch of the main road around Paley Woods. If I'm not mistaken, Tribble is loose around there. Get going. Singer should hurry. I'm on my way to the mill."

Tribble's pretty far from the mill, he thought. *Why is he walking around here? I wonder if he has realized yet that he stole the wrong horse? And if he has, then what did he do with Diablo?*

With a very uneasy feeling in the pit of his stomach, Howard Algrin stepped on the gas.

In his mind's eye he imagined Ricki terribly upset, and when he realized that he might have to tell her that her beloved horse – No! That just couldn't happen!

Algrin turned off the road and stopped the car beside a meadow. Then he jumped out and raced off without even taking the time to slam the car door shut.

It's a shame you can't drive there directly. I'm such an idiot – I should have driven to the mill from the other side, he thought as he ran along the narrow path. *And I'm out of shape, too.* After a few yards, the slightly overweight man was already out of breath and had to slow down.

But, panting and whistling like a steam engine, he forced himself to keep going. He made a silent promise to himself that in the future he would pay more attention to his health, and stop living on cheeseburgers, fries, and coffee.

He stopped for a moment to catch his breath, and the roof of the old mill became visible behind the trees. What was waiting for him there? Would Diablo still be alive? Would he even find him there, or had the anonymous phone caller just tried to send him on a false trail again?

Well, if he just stood there, he'd never find out! And, after all, he had seen Tribble.

He took a deep breath and started to run again.

Chapter 8

Ricki parked Gwendolyn's bike at the same place they'd rested their horses the previous day. As she turned toward the mill and entered the old building, her heart was pounding with excitement, anticipation – and apprehension. She had a peculiar feeling that Diablo was somewhere close by, watching her.

The door creaked as she opened it. Ricki walked a few feet inside the mill and peered intensely into all the corners and crevices.

Impossible, she thought. *There's not enough room for a horse inside this building.* There was too much clutter around the millstone, and it was decidedly too narrow for anyone to have led Diablo through the space.

Nevertheless, Ricki kept going. She assumed that the thieves would have wanted to find a hiding place that was almost inaccessible to others. However, after having gone through the entire building yesterday with Gwendolyn and looking everywhere inside, she knew, after only five minutes, that she was wasting precious time in this part of the building.

She stepped outside quickly and had to close her eyes for a moment, because the bright sunlight blinded her.

Now what? she pondered. *Where should I continue the search? Diablo could be anywhere!*

Somewhat indecisively, she gazed at the five sheds and buildings that surrounded the mill. They were all in a state of decay. And there was nothing but silence. Of course, the odds that she would find Diablo here were about one to – Agh! She didn't want to think about it.

Ricki bent down to pick up a stone. Suddenly she had the urge to throw her problems, together with the stone, as far away from her as possible. However, as she bent down she stopped short, puzzled.

"Huh, that wasn't here yesterday!" she murmured aloud as her eyes focused on a deep tire track that was pressed into the damp ground.

The girl swallowed excitedly. Was it possible after all, that Diablo ...?

She followed the tracks closely for a few yards and came to a place where the soil had been stamped down hard. The track marks of rather large shoes were easily visible as well as countless crescent-shaped tracks – horseshoes!

Slowly Ricki sank to her knees, laid her fingers carefully along the crescent shapes, and began to tremble with excitement. Their horses hadn't made these tracks yesterday when they visited the mill.

"Diablo," she whispered hoarsely. "He's here! I know it!"

Ricki looked back down at the ground and tried to figure out where her horse had been led. Soon she was able to determine which shed the tracks were leading to.

With a lump in her throat, she sensed that she was nearing the end of the search for her beloved horse. Nevertheless, she was too afraid just to run over to the half-caved-in shed and rush inside. Although that was what she wanted to do most of all, she had to deal with the possibility that the thieves were probably still there.

Why is everything so quiet? That's really strange, thought Ricki, and felt herself begin to panic. Diablo was not a calm, quiet horse. He had always made himself known loudly when he sensed that she was near.

My God, surely they wouldn't have hurt him, the girl thought, trying to reassure herself. But all of a sudden, the fear she felt for her beloved horse's well-being overcame any misgivings she might have had about her personal safety.

"Diablo," she called again, more loudly but still a little hesitantly, and then she inhaled deeply. "Diablo, where are you?" Her shout cut through the unnatural stillness that surrounded the old mill.

Ricki listened intently, but – much as she hoped for it – she heard no answering whinny from her horse.

*

Diablo twitched when he heard his friend's voice. Was this real? Had Ricki called to him? Or was he just dreaming? The black horse moved his ears, straining to hear everything outside the shed.

"Diablo ..." The sound came to him once again, and now he tried frantically to whinny, but with the cloth tied around his muzzle, he was able to let out only a muffled noise.

122

Desperately Diablo tensed his muscles and tried to get out from under the heavy metal railing that was lying on top of him. But it was useless, it didn't budge, and anyway, his front hoof was wedged inside the railing. He couldn't move.

Ricki thought she heard a faint metallic sound and raced toward the shed. Nothing and no one could hold her back now. "Diablo, I'm coming!" she called again and almost pushed in the rotted door, as she banged her body against it to get it open.

Her eyes needed a few seconds to adjust to the dusky light inside, but then she saw the extent of the precarious situation that Diablo was entangled in.

"Good grief, what ... what have they done to you?" Ricki's heart felt so heavy, she could hardly put one foot in front of the other.

"Diablo?" she called to him desperately. His complete lack of movement made her fear the worst, but when she heard his soft snorting, she ran to him at once.

Horrified, she stared at Diablo, and then she knelt close to him and laid a caressing hand on his thoroughly sweaty coat.

"Stay calm, my darling, everything's going to be okay. Don't be afraid. I'm going to get you out of here somehow."

First she leaned way over to Diablo's head and tried to tear off the cloth around his muzzle by reaching through the bars of the railing. But Tribble had also tied it to the halter. The knots were so tight that Ricki couldn't untie them, at least not from her current position.

Diablo began to breathe more and more heavily. Helplessly and trustingly, he kept his gaze on Ricki, who was trying to find her pocketknife somewhere in her jeans. No luck.

Desperate, she looked around the shed for a sharp object, but she couldn't find anything that looked as though it would do the job. Then she remembered that she'd seen a large knife on one of the shelves the previous day.

"Wait, Diablo, I'll be right back! In a minute, you'll be able to breathe normally again!" She got up quickly and ran off to retrieve the knife.

Awkwardly, but with great care, she inserted the blade of the knife under the cloth and began to saw back and forth, but the knife was so dull that it made her effort useless.

Agitatedly she threw the dull, rusted tool against the wall and returned to the tedious task of undoing the knots with her fingers while she talked soothingly to Diablo.

After a while, which seemed like an eternity to her, she was actually able to loosen the topknot, but if she needed the same amount of time for the remaining three ... Ricki felt a raging anger growing inside her. She leaned over as far as possible so that she could grip the material with both hands. She had to be careful not to put her weight on the upturned railing that was lying across Diablo's neck. With all her strength, she managed to loosen the cloth a little, and finally she was able to slide it over Diablo's nostrils.

Ricki took a deep breath, got up, and observed her horse, who had expanded his nostrils in order to take air into his lungs. When his breathing had at last returned to normal, he opened his mouth and kept sticking out his tongue.

Ricki understood. She jumped up again and looked around for a bucket or a tub, but when she didn't find anything right away, she ran outside. While on the run, she removed the sweatshirt she'd tied around her waist. Quickly she bent down at the stream and dipped the sweatshirt into the water.

When it was soaking wet, she pulled it back out, bunched it up to hold the moisture, and ran back to Diablo.

"Here, my good boy, I have something for you," she said, holding the soaking-wet sweatshirt in front of his muzzle. Greedily, the horse's parched lips and dry tongue pressed themselves into the dripping material.

At the same time, Ricki examined Diablo's situation more closely. It made her sick to imagine that the horse could panic and be even more seriously injured by the metal railing. Up to now, all she had noticed were a few scrapes, but she knew that the real danger was the imprisoned hoof.

Cautiously she walked around her black horse, who remained lying on the ground completely still, as though he sensed that any motion could make his situation worse.

Encouraged, Ricki grabbed the front hoof that was stuck between the railing bars and tried to free it by a twisting and tilting motion. But Diablo held the leg straight and stiff, and the girl had no chance to free the hoof.

After a few attempts, Ricki gave up, convinced that she would never manage to free her horse by herself. Desperate, she turned her gaze heavenward and asked for help.

Tortured by her helplessness, she looked down at Diablo. All she could do was remove the halter to give the horse more freedom of movement. Then the black horse would likely be able to work his way out from under the heavy metal railing; but since the front hoof was caught between the bars, he'd probably wind up injuring rather than freeing himself. Therefore, Ricki decided not to do that, but now she didn't know how to proceed. She knew she needed at least one more person to help her.

Since no one besides Chester knew where she had gone on the bike, and she had asked him to tell the others not to follow her, it was clear that she was pretty much on her own here.

"Diablo," she said quietly, "I hate to leave you alone, but I must if I'm going to be able to help you. Do you understand? I have to bike back to the farm and get help; otherwise you could be lying here forever! Oh, Diablo, I wish you could tell me what I should do!" Sobbing, she laid her face tenderly on Diablo's coat. She was at the end of her strength and hadn't even noticed that the shed door moved a bit.

"Oh, my goodness!" Howard Algrin exclaimed in shock when he found Ricki and Diablo lying on the ground. "Ricki? Ricki! It's you! My heavens, how did you get here? Are you and your horse okay?"

Ricki turned around startled and then breathed a sigh of relief when she recognized the Sheriff. Nevertheless, her heart was beating wildly. If that had been one of the thieves ...

"Sheriff Algrin, I am so glad to see you here. Diablo is caught in the railing, and I've tried, but ... and then –"

"Calm down, honey, calm down! Go slowly. We're going to get you and Diablo out of this mess. Let me see. Is he well trained, or should I worry about him kicking me in the head?"

Ricki shook her head wildly. "No, no, Diablo is the sweetest horse in the whole world!" she responded as Algrin quickly assessed the situation.

"We need a heavy bolt cutter and probably a knife, too. Look Ricki, my car is back there where the path ends on the meadow. Get on your bike and ride there. You'll find everything we need in the trunk."

Ricki looked back down at Diablo.

"You drive around with a bolt cutter?" she asked, incredulous.

Algrin nodded and shoved her out the door.

"It's part of the standard gear," he explained. "Now, get going, hurry.

Ricki raced over to where she had left Gwendolyn's bike, jumped on, and started to pedal furiously.

He's alive! The Sheriff will free him! Dear God, thank you so much!

*

"We'll take the horse trailer," Mrs. Highland announced. "Diablo will be glad when this is all over and he's home."

"Are you sure that Ricki's horse is really in the old mill?" Gwendolyn asked her grandmother.

"No, right now it's only a possibility! We'll only be sure when we see him in front of us. But Howard is checking up on a tip the police received."

"I hope so much, for Ricki's sake, that she gets her Diablo back," sighed Lillian as she ran behind Kevin and Cathy.

William drove the horse trailer into the courtyard. "So, come on, let's go!" Mrs. Highland climbed up onto the wide seat beside William and Gwendolyn, and the kids got in the back.

"Everybody in?" William looked at Eleanor Highland as she slammed the door shut.

"Yes. Please, hurry!"

"Do you think the thieves are still nearby?" asked Cathy nervously.

"How should we know? Cathy, don't ask such stupid questions!" Kevin tapped his forehead. He was overanxious and kept cracking his knuckles, which was really getting on Lillian's nerves.

"Will you stop that cracking? It's driving me crazy!"

"If you young people are going to fight the whole way there, I'm sorry you didn't stay behind! Pull yourselves together!" Mrs. Highland gave them a disapproving glance and the teens looked sheepishly at one another.

"I'm sorry," Lillian said immediately. Even Kevin mumbled a quiet, "sorry." Everyone stared, silently, out the windows.

"Turn right up there," said Gwendolyn, pointing through the window to the fork in the road that led to the old mill.

"I know," responded William, who knew all of the trails and roads around the farm like the back of his hand.

"Look, up there, isn't that Sheriff Algrin's car?" Gwendolyn sat up straight and gave her grandmother a little pinch in the arm.

"Could be. I'm glad that he's already there."

William stopped the trailer directly behind the Sheriff's car.

Everyone got out hurriedly, and while William was carefully locking all the doors, the kids and Mrs. Highland were already on their way to the mill.

*

"So, now, first let's cut this metal railing so your friend can stretch a little." Algrin had immediately taken the bolt cutter from Ricki when she returned and had gone straight to work.

128

"Come here, Ricki, and hold his leg still. We don't want him to pull it away before the bars have been cut!"

Diablo's owner nodded and held the ankle joint of her horse in both hands.

"Okay," she said hoarsely and observed how Algrin had to keep starting over. Sweat was running down the Sheriff's forehead as he concentrated, but finally the metal bars were cut in half with a loud crack, and Ricki carefully allowed Diablo's leg to glide into its natural position.

She ran quickly around her horse and began to tug at the halter in order to free his head as well.

"Wait, Ricki, we'll cut through that rope too. That will be quicker!" Algrin edged her aside and placed the sharp knife on the rope and quickly freed Diablo's head.

"So, now it's a little more complicated," he said and put the knife down. "Ricki, I'm going to try to lift the railing up high enough to allow him to slip his head out from underneath. But you have to pay attention if he gets up. As soon as he's standing, grab his halter and lead him two or three steps to the side, so that I can let it fall back down."

Diablo's owner nodded again.

"Stay calm, Diablo. It will be over soon. You're a very good boy, very good. Steady now..."

Algrin spit in his hands and went to work. "On the count of three: one ... two ... threeee!" With considerable exertion the Sheriff heaved the metal railing upward and groaned loudly, "All right, Diablo, hurry up, this thing is heavy." But the black horse just remained lying still on the floor.

"Diablo, hurry, get up, come on, let's go." Ricki was nearly out of control. Finally, she grabbed Diablo's halter and pulled on it with all her might, but Diablo didn't react.

129

"Get out of the way, Ricki. I can't hold this thing any longer!" shouted Algrin. The metal railing was beginning to slip out of his grasp. If the girl didn't get out of the way immediately, then ... "Get out of the way, Ricki!" he shouted again.

"No!" screamed the girl in panic, almost hysterical with fear that the railing would fall back down on her Diablo. "Diablo ... come on ... pleeease!"

Just at that moment, Mrs. Highland and the kids entered the shed. They stayed in the doorway, shocked at what they saw. Only William reacted immediately. He jumped over Diablo with a huge leap, and, without even thinking, grabbed the metal railing and took most of the weight off Algrin.

At the same time, Diablo finally seemed to be waking up from his benumbed condition. He made two tries and then rolled onto his belly, stretched out his front legs, and pushed himself upright.

Ricki hung onto his halter and pulled him back violently, at least two yards, so that the men could let the railing fall crashing to the floor.

Scared to death, Diablo jumped to the side with his owner, and stood there trembling.

"Ugh," groaned Algrin and rubbed his fiery red hands. "That was really close! Thanks, William! Another second or two and I shudder to think what would have happened!"

William grinned. "We have Mrs. Highland to thank for that," he said. "She told me to ignore the speed limit and get here as fast as possible."

They all looked over at Ricki, who was sobbing quietly into Diablo's mane. The girl was obviously physically and emotionally drained.

The girl's friends had tears in their eyes as well. They all felt very close to her, though no one went to her to give her a hug. They didn't want to intrude on Ricki and her horse at this moment of joyful reunion.

Mrs. Highland, however, felt no such reservation and walked straight toward the two of them. She checked the horse quickly, running her hands over his legs. To her delight, Diablo appeared not to have sustained any injuries.

"It's over, child," she said in a trembling yet calming voice. "Thank God, you have him back. And as far as I can judge, he's okay. The scrapes are minor and will heal in a few days."

Lovingly, she laid her hands on Ricki's shoulders and was touched that the girl leaned back into her, exhausted.

"He was really lucky, wasn't he?" stammered Ricki as she looked at Diablo thorough a thick veil of tears.

"Yes," nodded Mrs. Highland, "the thieves –"

"I don't mean the thieves. The railing could have crushed him," Ricki struggled to explain.

"Yes, Ricki, it could have killed him, but there was a powerful guardian angel standing nearby who prevented him from getting seriously injured," answered Eleanor Highland. Then she asked William to lead Diablo to the trailer.

"No!" Ricki stared at Mrs. Highland with huge eyes. "I want to lead him myself. He ... I'm so happy, I ... I just can't let go of him right now."

"It's okay, Ricki, you take him outside. We brought a horse trailer with us."

Mrs. Highland gestured to the other teenagers to give Ricki and Diablo some room. Obediently they all stepped to the side.

131

"Bring your boy home safely, Ricki," Algrin called after her.

Ricki turned to the Sheriff. "Thank you," she said softly. "Thanks a million. I'll never forget what you did." Then she left the shed with her horse.

"I've never seen such a look of gratitude before," sniffed Algrin, overcome by Ricki's heartfelt emotions.

William patted the Sheriff amiably on the shoulder. "Well," he said, trying to cover Algrin's embarrassment, "Gwendolyn has some very special friends, but that's no reason for you to get sentimental in your old age!"

"And they say policemen don't have any feelings," Eleanor teased him, and then she took her old friend's hand in hers and held it tight. "A sincere thank you from me as well, Howard. Without you, this whole thing could have ended quite differently."

The Sheriff took a deep breath, gently kissed Eleanor's hand before letting go, and reached into the pocket of his jacket.

"What are you doing?" she asked.

"First I'm going to send for my colleagues in forensics, and then I'm going to drive to the station. I want to see if they've arrested Tribble yet."

"Tribble?" Eleanor asked in bewilderment.

"That's the guy who probably stole Diablo. He's not unknown to me, by the way," he explained.

Mrs. Highland nodded at him, satisfied. "Good, and we'll make sure that Ricki and Diablo get back to the estate with no more incidents."

Algrin nodded and pulled out his cell phone to call his colleagues.

In the doorway of the shed, Mrs. Highland turned around

and smiled warmly at her old friend. "Remember what I said about free dinners for the rest of your life? I meant that!"

Algrin grinned and nodded to her to show that he had understood, although he was already speaking with Sam French about the case.

*

Diablo's return didn't prove to be as uncomplicated as Mrs. Highland had hoped.

He reacted very strongly to the trailer when he saw it at the end of the path. He seemed to associate the vehicle with the last tortuous hours, and he stubbornly refused to go any nearer than ten yards. No, he would never get back into such a vehicle.

Ricki coaxed and coaxed him, but Diablo showed the whites of his eyes and flattened his ears back in warning. When Ricki tried to tug at his halter, he snapped at her arm and glared at her angrily.

Ricki was scared. "What did they do to him?" she asked tonelessly, staring at her beloved horse in disbelief. Diablo had never tried to bite her before.

"Maybe it would work better if you lead him with a rope, instead of holding onto his halter directly," suggested Kevin, but Lillian interjected, "He'll have even more head freedom that way!"

"Maybe ..." Cathy had just taken a deep breath when Mrs. Highland gave her a sign to leave Ricki alone.

"Children, you can say what you want, but this horse isn't going to get into a horse trailer today! Maybe to-morrow things will be different, but today ... Diablo is in shock. That's why he's behaving like he is with Ricki."

"So now what?" Ricki asked as she observed her horse.

"There's no help for it. We'll have to take him back home on foot."

"We'll go with you," Lillian said softly, and Cathy and Gwendolyn nodded in agreement.

Kevin went up to Ricki. "You can drive back with William, if you want. You're completely exhausted! I'll bring Diablo home," he offered his girlfriend, but even as he was walking toward her, Diablo snorted nervously and danced backward.

"Come on, Diablo, you know me! Calm down, I'm not going to hurt you." Kevin spoke quietly and calmly to the animal, but Diablo just became more and more upset, so that Ricki had trouble keeping him in check.

"Stand still, please, Kevin! I think it's better if I take him home. Please, I think I'd rather go by myself. He'll probably be less upset than if you guys all come with me!"

"I think you're right, Ricki, but I'm uneasy about leaving you alone with Diablo in his condition," said Mrs. Highland. "At least let Kevin follow you. He can leave sufficient distance between you so that Diablo won't feel threatened."

Ricki nodded and gave in, although she didn't really think it was such a good idea.

*

After William and Mrs. Highland and her friends had slowly driven away, Ricki began to walk toward the estate.

134

She talked to her horse continuously and told him all kinds of things, like she always did. Diablo, however, didn't react to anything she said.

He kept trying to break loose and continued to look at her doubtfully with his ears laid back. Then Kevin, who was walking some distance behind them, sneezed loudly. The black horse jumped to the side unexpectedly, turned on his hind legs, and reared up aggressively.

Ricki was terribly upset about her horse's reaction, but she forced herself not to let go of the rope.

Diablo stared down at her as though she were an enemy. Furiously, he scraped his front hoof, which had been injured slightly on the side by the metal railing, into the ground on the gravel path.

Suddenly, Ricki became aware of an unsettling feeling growing inside her. As she observed Diablo's angry expression and aggressive behavior, she realized, with horror, that it was fear she was feeling – fear of her own horse. For the first time in her young life, she was afraid of Diablo.

Chapter 9

Ricki tried to calm herself. She knew that when people become afraid they give off a particular scent that horses can detect. It was clear to her that Diablo could literally smell her deepest feelings. She swallowed hard and noticed that her hand had begun to tremble.

"Diablo," she said as casually as she could. "Don't do anything stupid! We're going home, and then you can relax in your own stall. I'm sure that you'll feel much better tomorrow. But right now we have to keep going. Come on!" Ricki tugged on his halter but Diablo bit his lips angrily and took three steps backward as he focused his eyes on the girl.

All of a sudden he whinnied loudly and reared up again, and this time he tore the rope out of Ricki's hand.

He turned abruptly and thundered off.

"No, Diablo, not again!" Ricki shouted in panic. "Kevin, for heaven's sakes, catch him!" But who could stop a bolting horse?!

Diablo raced toward the boy and dashed past him, just missing him by a hair. The horse appeared to be headed back toward the old mill.

Ricki ran after him for a few yards, but before she even reached Kevin, her strength gave out and she collapsed on the ground, sobbing.

*

Diablo had picked up the scent of the mares and foals on the Montvale paddock when Ricki was leading him toward the horse trailer. He was also aware of the nervous whinnying of his fellow horses, who were clustering together in fear on their meadow.

The black horse became more and more anxious with every step he took, because he sensed that these animals were in danger. On the other hand, Ricki and the others were still too involved in what had already happened to pay attention to the whinnying of the horses standing so far away.

Since horses are, by nature, herd animals, Diablo instinctively picked up on the other horses' sense of alarm and just had to go to their aid. Only he didn't know how he could let Ricki know, so he had refused to enter the horse trailer.

Later, as his two-legged friend kept leading him farther away from the frightened animals, there was nothing else he could do but tear himself away from her.

*

Ricki needed only a few minutes to get herself under control again.

"What in the world is the matter with Diablo?" she kept asking, but Kevin couldn't give her any answers. Instead he stressed the urgency of the situation.

"We've got to go after him right away, otherwise we'll have to begin the whole search all over again," he said.

Ricki nodded. "You're right, but we'll never be able to catch him," she said with resignation.

"Right! As long as we stay here doing nothing, we won't even be able to tell in which direction he's going!"

Kevin held out his hand to Ricki and pulled her up from the ground.

"Okay," she sniffed, and then the two started running after Diablo.

*

"They should be here by now, shouldn't they?" Lillian kept glancing at her watch and was getting nervous.

"Don't get all stressed out. Maybe Diablo's joints are hurting and they have to take a lot of breaks," Gwendolyn tried to distract her friend.

"Yeah, that's possible," agreed Cathy, but Lillian was becoming even more upset.

"And I'm telling you guys, something's wrong!" she claimed for the third time. "I know your grandmother means well and that she is genuinely concerned for our safety, but I'm going to start walking toward them. I have to know what's happening! Are you coming with me?"

"Of course, if you think something's wrong." Cathy stood up right away and Gwendolyn got up as well.

"Should we go on horseback?" Gwen asked. "It would be a lot faster than if we went on foot."

"That's true, but maybe Diablo would get even more upset if the other horses got near him," Lillian objected.

"Or maybe not," Gwendolyn replied. "After all, he's had nothing but bad experiences with people, but not with other horses!"

"That's true, too! Okay, let's get our horses saddled."

The girls ran toward the stable and, a few minutes later, they were on their way.

The closer they came to the mill, the more the girls rocked back and forth in their saddles in agitation. There was still no sign of Ricki, Diablo, or Kevin.

"Now *I'm* beginning to think something's happened," Gwendolyn admitted unhappily as they turned onto the meadow that led to the mill path.

"Shh! Be quiet!" she hissed suddenly, and stopped her Black Jack, who was twitching his ears attentively.

"Did you hear that?" she asked, but both Cathy and Lillian shook their heads no.

"What?"

"It sounded like a strange scream, but somehow not human."

"What do you mean?"

"Oh, don't ask me! I have no idea. Maybe I was wrong ..."

But Lillian suddenly interrupted her. "There! Now I heard it, too!" Lillian gazed back and forth. "Where did that come from?"

"I think from back there," said Cathy, pointing at a little grove of trees.

"From there? Are you sure?" Gwendolyn looked at her friend doubtfully, but she nodded.

"I think so," she replied.

"Hmm, over there, behind the trees is the Montvales' paddock. They usually have their mares and their foals on that meadow. Maybe we should ride over there quickly and check it out, to make sure nothing's happened. After all, the paddock is quite a distance from the main house at the farm!" suggested Gwendolyn.

"I thought we were looking for Ricki!" said Lillian with some annoyance. She had the feeling that Gwendolyn was more worried about the Montvale horses than she was about Ricki, who should have been back long ago.

"Ricki is over there, too," Cathy yelled all of a sudden, and gave Rashid a sign to gallop from a standing position. She had just heard Ricki calling Diablo, and the faint sound was coming from the direction of the inhuman scream as well.

Without questioning her further, Lillian galloped after her on Doc Holliday. Only Gwendolyn paused a moment before she understood.

"Come on, Black Jack," she shouted to her horse. "Show me what you can do!" and with that, she was on her way to the Montvale paddock as well.

*

Diablo raced back over the distance he had covered with Ricki earlier. Before coming to the path that led to the mill, he turned off in order to gallop directly toward the paddock through the thick trees.

He could hear the frightened snorts and whinnies of the horses more clearly now, and also the scream of a mare who had positioned herself in front of her foal to protect him.

Diablo's instincts told him that he had no time to lose and, stretching himself almost flat, he began to gallop over the soft ground of the woods.

A short time later, he had reached his goal. He whinnied threateningly as he thundered out of the woods and slid to a stop.

"What's that?" Baffled, a young man turned around. He was standing only a few yards from a small white dappled mare who was protectively standing in front of her weeks-old foal.

There was a coarsely woven rope around the foal's neck. It was tied to the fence. Every time the foal moved, he scraped the tender skin around his neck on the rope. The mare's white coat had turned red around the croup. Blood was running from a long, thin cut that went from the hipbone to her mane. Her entire back leg was covered in blood.

The man's confusion disappeared when he saw that the relatively high fence around the paddock separated him from the black devil that had suddenly appeared. He grinned coldly.

Slowly he turned back to the mare, who was looking at him with frightened eyes, while the foal pressed himself against her in terror.

"So, you little piece of garbage, let's see how you like this ..." In slow motion, he raised his arm, and Diablo saw a six-foot pole, at the end of which something metal was reflecting in the sun.

The knife was tied on tightly and could stab or cut, whichever the man chose. This handmade lance was the weapon of the horse butcher, and he had chosen the beautiful white mare and her foal as his next victims.

Diablo smelled the mare's blood and sensed that the man who was standing over there was responsible for that animal's suffering. All of a sudden, the black horse neighed loudly, full of hate.

He reared up powerfully on his hind legs and pawed the air before he ran back and gathered his strength and focused on the fence. Then he raced toward the fence in a full gallop. At the last minute, he sprang, pulled in his hips, and then set down incredibly lightly inside the wooden fence.

The man heard Diablo's hoofbeats, but he was sure that they came from outside the paddock. He didn't even turn around; he just kept concentrating on his victim.

The little mare pushed her foal slightly to one side, as Diablo approached. He bumped against the horse butcher as he ran past him, knocking him off balance and almost to the ground.

Horrified, the evil young man stared at the large black horse, who had turned and was galloping straight at him again.

Suddenly the man straightened up. His eyes blazed, and it was obvious that he was excited by the idea that he could hurt this powerful creature who was attacking him so bravely.

Diablo came closer and closer, and with each step he took, the man raised the lance a bit higher, until he held it as high as Diablo's breast.

"Come on, you devil!" the man taunted in an ice-cold voice. "It's your own fault! I don't care who dies, you or the other ones. Come on, keep coming!"

And Diablo kept coming toward him.

*

Ricki and Kevin had run all the way back and, from a distance, had seen Diablo disappear between the trees.

When they got to the place where they had last seen him, they heard Diablo's tense whinnying, as he answered the mare.

Diablo's voice went right through Ricki, and suddenly she understood that Diablo had had a reason for bolting.

"I don't know what's going on, but I have the feeling that it's something bad," she panted, out of breath.

Kevin nodded. "You know what?!" he said. "Run back to the mill and get the Sheriff as a backup. I'll run after Diablo, okay?"

Ricki shook her head. "No! I'm going after Diablo!" And with that, she took off.

Kevin rolled his eyes. Why did Ricki always have to have her own way?

He didn't feel easy about it as he ran toward the mill, but when he saw Howard Algrin, only a few minutes later, he calmed down.

"Sheriff! Sheriff!" he shouted from a distance.

"Who's that? ... Kevin? What are you doing here? I thought you would have been back at the estate a long time ago!" Algrin stared at him attentively, but when Kevin reported what had happened, the Sheriff moved immediately.

"Come on. Where did you say Diablo ran off to?"

"Through the little grove of trees."

"Aha!"

Together they hurried back down the trail to the Sheriff's car, where, out of breath, they sat down heavily on the seats.

"Please, drive fast," pleaded Kevin, who couldn't stop worrying about Ricki and Diablo.

Cathy raced on Rashid through the woods, followed by Lillian and Gwendolyn on their horses.

A few moments earlier, she had seen the Sheriff's car on a side road going pretty fast, and she thought that it was somehow connected to Diablo.

She kept urging her horse to give everything he had, and she managed to get to the Montvale paddock at the same time that the Sheriff and Kevin arrived in the car.

She reined in Rashid hard, and stared in horror at the middle of the paddock, where Ricki, screaming, was running toward a man who was holding a lance aimed directly at Diablo.

"What's going on?" shouted Lillian, out of breath, as she brought Holli to a stop. Gwendolyn was about to ask the same thing, when she saw Cathy's horrified gaze. It was answer enough.

"Good grief!" whispered Gwendolyn tonelessly and as white as a sheet. "The ... the horse butcher!"

Algrin and Kevin had jumped out of the car, and as the Sheriff raced toward the paddock, he called a warning to Kevin, "Don't even think about running after me!"

Ricki's friend stopped short and stood still, watching the scene unfold before him as though through a heavy fog.

Diablo, who had instinctively judged the danger of the long pointed object the man was holding in his hand, had stopped a few yards in front of him and observed the man closely, as he slowly approached him.

"You're a coward, horse!" the man taunted the animal in a sneering tone. "So huge ... so strong ... and as cowardly as a rabbit! Stand still, now, so that I can get you good!"

Diablo's ears twitched back and forth. He pawed the earth with his front hoof in indecision. Suddenly, his head jolted upward, because he had been distracted by Ricki, who was screaming and running at the man from behind.

"No!" she screamed. "Leave my horse alone, you freak! Diablo, run! Get away from here!"

The black horse kept staring at his owner, then he decided to go over to her.

"Go away, Diablo! Run!" Ricki shouted, but Diablo didn't understand what she wanted.

The man's steely grin morphed into an evil sneer. "Yes!" he screamed, completely insane. "Just keep coming!"

Ricki had finally reached the deranged man. She ran into him with all of the force from the run and wrapped her arms around his neck.

"Leave my horse alone!" she screamed into his ears, using all her strength to pull his head back. But the horse butcher just twisted back and forth and shook her off as though she were nothing more than an annoying fly.

Ricki stumbled and fell, but before she could get up again, the man had turned and was now menacing her with his lance.

"I don't want to hurt you," he said in a strange voice. "But this horse ... these beasts ... they are all creatures from hell! They must be destroyed, do you understand me? Destroyed!"

Paralyzed with fear, Ricki didn't dare move, as the man's glassy eyes seemed to gaze into nothing.

"Get away from the girl! Don't you dare do anything to her!" Howard Algrin was only about ten yards away when

145

Diablo started moving. He had watched in a rage as this man had flung Ricki to the ground and pointed that awful weapon at her.

The black horse whinnied shrilly. Nobody was allowed to hurt his beloved Ricki – no one!

With a few gallops, the horse reached the man and brushed into him so that he lost his balance and dropped the lance.

Diablo stopped short, turned around on his hind legs, and reared straight up, his front hooves whirling in the air. A hair's breath away from the man, he set his hooves down hard, before rearing up again.

The horse butcher rolled to the side hastily to avoid being crushed by the raging horse and landed directly in front of Algrin's feet.

The Sheriff rammed his knee into the man's back, twisted his arms backward, and snapped a pair of handcuffs on him. Ricki got up quickly and grabbed Diablo's halter.

"Calm down, my darling, calm down, it's over! He can't hurt you anymore. That's a good boy." She spoke to him in a trembling voice and was relieved to see that Diablo reacted to her voice just as he had in the past.

All of the hate and rage had disappeared from the black horse's eyes, and he poked her in the chest with a tender-brusque gesture, almost taking Ricki's breath away.

She began to laugh and realized, to her great joy, that her fear of Diablo had vanished into thin air. Happy, she gave him a hug, and then led him away from the paddock.

She glanced at the mare with her sweet foal, and all of a sudden she noticed the injury on the little horse's hindquarters.

"The little white mare is injured," she called to Kevin, who came running up to her.

"Are you okay? And Diablo, too?" He looked at his girlfriend with concern, and she nodded hastily.

"Yeah! Look at the mare. She's more important right now! See if the injury's serious!" she begged the boy. However, when the boy tried to approach the two animals, they ran away.

"I'm going to ride to the Montvales' house and tell them," shouted Gwendolyn, who was relieved to see that both Ricki and Diablo had come through this awful experience unscathed, and also that the horse butcher had finally been captured. Now her grandmother's farm and all the horse farms in the area could get some peace.

Cathy and Lillian, also relieved at the outcome, nodded to Ricki as she and Diablo left the paddock together. They had so much to tell their girlfriend, but they were just too shaken up to be able to say anything.

"Let's get out of here," said Ricki softly. Now that is was all over, her legs had begun to tremble. She gave Diablo's halter a slight tug, and he trotted after her, as gentle as a lamb.

*

"Well, that von Branden is a real tough cookie," reported Howard Algrin, who was seated next to Mrs. Highland at the dinner table and just about to take another slice of roast beef from the platter. "He still hasn't confessed, although Tribble has already told us everything. Von Branden must have ordered the horse kidnapping right after you refused to sell him Garibaldi. I still don't know how

Tribble knew all about the alarm system here, but I'll find out! By the way, Tribble had an accomplice who made an anonymous phone call to tell us about the mill. He must have had some reason to want to revenge himself on Tribble."

"How do you know that?" Mrs. Highland was curious to find out.

"Well, it's simple. Tribble informed us about Mac – that's the name of the accomplice – and we caught up with him at the airport, before he could get away. The two of them have committed quite a few burglaries. However, both of them say that von Branden put them up to it. I'll have to question that gentleman again tomorrow. I'm positive I'll get him to crack!" Algrin grinned and helped himself to some more mashed potatoes.

"It's delicious, eating a real dinner. Certainly a different experience from the usual french fries and hotdogs!"

"Does anyone know if the white mare was seriously injured?" Ricki asked, still worried about her. Gwendolyn shook her head.

"Chester met with Mr. Montvale this evening. The vet said she had been lucky, and that the cut is relatively superficial."

"Thank heaven!" Ricki sighed.

"I would never have imagined that von Branden was involved in all this," exclaimed Mrs. Highland, shaking her head. "That means that Ricki was right when she said she recognized the voice on the taped phone call."

"Yes, and even if he remains stubborn and doesn't confess, the tape of that phone call is going to make the case against him! What an idiot! At least now we know how he accumulated so much money in the bank. He isn't a wealthy

148

businessman, just simply a thief and a fraud who has stolen millions over the years!" grinned Algrin.

"Boy, am I glad this day is over," sighed Kevin.

"Me, too," agreed Lillian. "I didn't think it was possible to experience so many horrible things in so short a period of time."

"I hope that now, finally, there will be some peace and quiet around here," responded Cathy as she swallowed the last bite of her dinner.

"Let's hope so, my child!" Mrs. Highland was smiling, but the worries that she had had in the last few hours for Ricki and Diablo, and all of her horses, were still etched into her face.

"What's going to happen to the horse butcher?" Kevin looked at Algrin anxiously.

"I'm not certain yet what will happen to him," he said. "We still have a lot to learn about this case. He really seems to be mentally ill, and if that's the case, he will probably be committed into an institution, but that still has to be decided. And it seems to be an odd coincidence, the two horse crimes happening concurrently in the same geographical area. We think von Branden might have used that to his advantage."

"The main thing is that the horse butcher can't do any more harm!" Kevin announced.

"Well, we owe that to Diablo. With that horse's help we were able to catch him," the Sheriff said, smiling at Ricki. "Your horse found a special way to thank us for saving him, didn't he?"

Ricki nodded. "That's true! And to think that I doubted him! I should have known that something was wrong when he acted that way."

"Yes, there's always something new to learn," the Sheriff observed wisely.

"Hey," responded Gwendolyn, changing the subject. "What do you guys want to do tomorrow? Do you feel like going to the movies, or would you rather go swimming? Or we could –"

Ricki cleared her throat softly. "Gwen," she interrupted her friend, and gazed at her and the other kids. "Would you be ... that is, would you guys be mad at me, if I told you that ... that I really want to go home tomorrow? I ... Diablo ..." Ricki paused; she couldn't find the right words.

For a moment, there was silence at the table.

Gwendolyn exchanged a glance with her grandmother, Lillian gave Cathy a look, and Kevin squeezed Ricki's hand tightly under the table.

"That's okay," answered Gwendolyn, and tried to hide her disappointment. She would have liked to keep her friends at Highland Farms forever. "You'll come back, won't you?"

Ricki nodded and swallowed a few tears. She really liked this girl, but more than ever, she longed for the peace and the security she knew were waiting for her at home.

"Of course, we'll come back," answered Lillian, and she had to admit that she, too, was looking forward to sleeping in her own bed again.

"But first, Gwen has to come and visit us," said Cathy grinning. "Black Jack can share a stall with Chico."

"Chico? Who's that?" asked Gwen, puzzled.

"Lillian's little donkey," explained Kevin and gave Ricki a kiss on her cheek.

"A donkey! Oh, how cute!" Gwendolyn beamed at her grandmother. "Grandma, don't we have room for –"

150

"No, Gwendolyn, please, no donkey on my estate!" Eleanor Highland made such a face that they all burst out laughing.

*

"Well, then, good luck, you kids, and many, many thanks for everything," said Mrs. Highland, as she said good-bye to Ricki and the others. She gave each one of them a hug. "You're welcome here any time."

"Oh, man, I'm really going to miss you guys," sniffed Gwendolyn, hugging her friends who, one by one, climbed into the front cab of the horse trailer, where William was waiting to take them home.

"Don't worry, you'll never get rid of us now," said Lillian. Ricki slammed the door of the vehicle so loudly that Diablo, in the back of the van, whinnied his disapproval.

"Your parents will probably think twice before letting you come back here," speculated Gwendolyn, recalling everything that had occurred.

"Why?" Kevin made a bewildered face. "Did something bad happen here?"

"Well – "

"Well, I don't know of anything," grinned Ricki out of the window. "How about you guys?"

"Nope!" shouted Lillian and Cathy, before they started to laugh merrily.

"And Diablo won't tell," added Ricki, as William started the engine. "Unless they bribe him with carrots and treats!" The girl laughed and squeezed Gwendolyn's hand once more. "See you, Gwen. Give little Golden Star a cuddle for me, and Sunshine and Garibaldi, too! Thanks

151

for everything," she called as William steered the trailer out of the yard.

"We should thank you," answered Gwendolyn quietly, before she ran over to the mares' stable to give Golden Star a hug, just as Ricki had asked her to.